hamishspiers.com

THE SUN ALWAYS SETS

Hamish Spiers

ISBN: 9780992370688

First Edition: 2019

10 9 8 7 6 5 4 3 2 1

This book is dedicated to, among others, my wife Erin and my son Jason.

It's also dedicated to all the folk out there who prefer their vampires, both the evil and the heart of gold varieties, a little more on the dangerous side.

Sunday

"You can't shelter me from the world forever, Mom."

Liz Garnier nodded as she looked around her adopted daughter's new place. "You've got me there, Portia."

Her daughter smiled, her almond eyes lit up with excitement. "But come on... What do you think?"

"It's nice," Liz admitted. "And I like what you've done with it." Feeling more was called for, she looked around for something else to comment on before settling on the furnishings. "This sofa's nice."

"Thanks. Also, you've got to admit the location's all right. It's a nice street and it's close to the college."

"Well, yeah," Liz conceded. "But so's our old place."

For a few moments, neither mother nor daughter said anything.

Portia sighed. "I know. It's not going to be the same." She gave her mother another smile, though this one had a tinge of sadness in it. "But I think it's time. I've got to start taking care of myself eventually. And I can't keep moving towns every second year just because you get a new job."

Liz nodded. She had her there. Spain. England. Switzerland. Slovakia. Moldavia. And now here on the western coast of the United States. And with her Spanish looks, Portia had a chance of passing herself off as Latin American and blending in a bit. She was even picking up the accent.

"And it's all part of growing up, isn't it?" her daughter added.

She had her there too, Liz knew. But for Portia, growing up was going to be a lot more than getting her own place, going to college and all those usual things. Sooner or later, whether a year from now or thirty, Portia would learn the truth about her. And after that, nothing would be the way it was.

Liz had always thought she understood what that meant. Now she wasn't so sure.

Monday

ARRIVING A FEW MINUTES BEFORE THE morning lecture began, Portia took her customary seat and watched as the other students filed into the hall. She smiled as she saw Jay Evans, a reasonably attractive friend, with sunkissed olive skin and great hair, but a bit of a goof.

"Hey, Portia," he said, sitting down on her left.

"Hey, Jay. What's up?"

"Not much."

Another friend—acquaintance really—sat in front of them and looked back with a grin. Matt Decker, sandy blonde and bright eyed. "Hey gang. Miss me?"

"What time did you get home last night, Matt?" Jay asked. "Four a.m. or something?"

Matt shrugged. "Technically morning but about then." He looked at Portia. "Hey, where's your Mom?"

Portia sighed. "She'll be here. The lecture hasn't started, Matt."

"Oh. Maybe I can quickly do the reading then."

Jay chuckled. "You suck, Matt. How'd you get in?"

Matt shrugged. "I test well. By the way, I think you left that party way too early. There was this one girl—"

Portia tuned out. Matt's party stories never did much for her. Maybe she needed a few female friends.

She looked around. There were a handful of girls around the room but everyone was already in their established groups. And as she counted the fifty or so students in the room, Portia realized the College of Palm Beach was pretty small. Maybe not the smallest college in the country as Jay claimed but it was a far cry from most of them.

Then she saw her mom by the entrance to the hall, lecture notes under one arm, jet black hair cut just above the shoulders, and sporting a black singlet top and tight fitting black jeans.

She was talking to a girl she hadn't seen before. European by her looks, with an alabaster complexion, dark auburn hair and amazing brown eyes.

Portia frowned. Why had that last thought popped into her head? It wasn't as though she was attracted to this girl.

"New student?" she wondered aloud.

"Oh, yeah?" Matt said, having a look. "I heard about her."

"Yeah, me too," Jay said. "She's Austrian. Or German or Swiss or something."

"Czech," Matt told him. "But nice try. You know, I think the geography department's still taking enrolments if you're interested. You've clearly got the stuff."

"Okay, guys," Portia said. "Knock it off. Mom's coming."

Sure enough, Liz was walking to the front of the lecture hall and the new girl, Portia noticed, was coming to sit nearby.

"Hey," Matt said, "I was thinking. If Liz is your mom, how's she going to grade you objectiv—"

Portia put her foot in the back of his chair.

Then Liz's smooth clear voice cut through the din in the room. "All right, everyone. I hope you enjoyed that reading on genre conventions. Today, we're looking at the..."

Portia listened carefully to every word of the lecture, noting the references her mom recommended, nodding along and laughing at her quips with the other students. But when it was over, she felt a bit sad.

She'd thought she'd be happy living away from home, being on her own. But the truth was she already missed her mom. And it wasn't as though she could hang out with her on campus. Mom had other classes to teach. Papers to grade. And Portia had her own studies too. Then there was the issue of Jay and Matt. If she hung out with her mom, they'd either make fun of her or tag along. And neither of those options was appealing.

"Now," Liz said, "I've still got a few more papers to get through but I like what I've read so far. And I'll let you know your results next week. All right, everyone. Take care and don't forget the reading. It'll rock your little worlds."

Portia put on a smile as she closed her notebook and put her stuff away. Around her, the other students in the lecture hall were all getting up to clear the room for the next class. Jay had climbed over the chair in front and was talking nonsense with Matt. And...

"Excuse me."

She turned around and saw the new girl.

"Hey."

The girl extended a hand. "Hey. I'm Ivana. Ivana Kovac."

"Portia Garnier. You're enrolled here?"

"Uh," Ivana hesitated. "What's the expression? I'm in the process."

"Your accent," Portia said, feigning surprise. "European?"

"Yeah."

"German?"

Ivana shook her head. "Czech."

So Matt had been right, Portia thought. It was known to happen sometimes.

"Although I've lived in Germany for a little bit," Ivana added. "Denmark. Norway. The UK for about six months. My mother and I move around a lot."

"Sounds like an interesting way to live."

Ivana shrugged. "If you don't mind being ditched on your own while your mother takes off for three months."

"She *does* that?"

"Oh, yeah. She's ditched me *now*."

Portia frowned. "Why?"

Ivana shrugged. "Traveling. Maybe hooking up with some boyfriend she doesn't want me to meet. I don't care."

"But she's your *mother*, right? She brought you into the world. Raised you?" Portia was painfully aware as she said this that she'd never known her birth mother, the poor woman who'd brought *her* into the world.

"Yeah, I know," Ivana replied. "I'll get her back one day."

Portia chuckled. "You're a bit... different, Ivana. I've got to say."

Ivana shrugged again. "I get that a lot. Anyway, the thing is I need a place to stay and I've got no clue where to begin. It sounds like the on campus accommodation is all taken and I don't know where to start looking for accommodation *off* campus so—"

"You could stay with me for a while," Portia offered. "I live a few blocks away but it's only a short bus ride and the walk's not much longer."

"Oh, I wouldn't want to be an imposition," Ivana started. "If you just—"

"Oh, it'd be no imposition," Portia insisted. "You know, I think it'd be... nice."

A few hours later, she was on the thin patch of lawn outside her place with Ivana behind her. "Well," she said. "This is it. It's not big but I've got two rooms. I don't have a spare bed but I've got a camping mattress you can use."

Ivana smiled. "Fine by me. It sounds great. Really."

Portia returned the smile as she opened the door and went in. When she put her bag down, she noticed Ivana was still outside.

"Don't be shy. Come in."

Ivana followed her, looking around the place. Her gaze fell on an acoustic guitar in a corner of the room.

"You play?" she asked.

Portia glanced at it. "Oh, that? Yeah. A little." She felt a bit bashful. "I'm not very good." She went over to her kitchen counter. She had a few sheets of paper with some chords and lyrics she'd written out. She tried to put them away without drawing attention but Ivana saw them straightaway.

"Oh, you write songs too?" She reached over. "Can I see?"

Portia still felt a little overwhelmed but she passed the sheets across.

"Wow," Ivana said, flipping through them. "I'd love to hear you play one of these."

However, this was all getting a bit too much for Portia. "Maybe some other time," she said, taking them back and putting them in a drawer. "How about a cup of coffee?"

Unlike Portia, Jay had a tutorial that evening so he didn't come home until a little later. Not that he minded. Matt was in the same class and they always had a freshly baked oven pizza from the cafeteria afterward. So evening classes had their perks.

Now he was cruising at a leisurely pace down a wide suburban street, with leafy trees over the sidewalk on each side. Then, seeing something on the right, he pulled over and got out of the car.

On the opposite sidewalk, a teenage boy was lying on his back, arms folded across his chest with a serene smile on his lips.

Jay crossed the street.

"Hey, kid," he said. "You all right?"

The boy didn't twitch.

Jay crouched down. "You don't want to talk? That's fine. But you can't just lie in..." He trailed off as he got a better look at the kid.

The boy's skin was white, almost blue. There were no signs of breathing. No rising and falling of the chest. And on his neck were two puncture wounds.

Jay staggered back and covered his mouth with one hand, fighting a sudden rush of nausea.

"Oh, fuck," he muttered, fumbling in his pocket for his phone.

A few blocks away, Liz was having a coffee at home with Natasha, a colleague who appeared to be of similar age, with shoulder length ash blonde hair and piercing blue eyes.

"How's Portia going, by the way?" her friend asked, taking a sip of her drink.

"She's going well," Liz said. "She's just moved into a new place so it's going to be a bit of an adjustment for the both of us. But I think we'll be all right."

"Of course you will," Natasha told her. "It's just another one of life's stages. That's all."

Liz nodded. "Yeah." She put her cup down. "By the way, I had this prospective student in my class today. Ivana Kovac."

Natasha frowned. "Can't say I know her."

"No, that's all right. But I thought you might be able to help me. I want to send her some information about the course but she's left an incorrect address with student records. And she doesn't seem to answer her phone."

"I wouldn't worry about it then. I mean, if she's not enrolled..."

"Oh, I'm not worried," Liz said, stretching the truth out like a rubber band. "But if you hear anything..."

"Sure," Natasha said. "I'll let you know."

At the Palm Beach police station, Kyle Destri sat alone away from his colleagues. In other circles, the athletically built, dark and handsome man could have been the center of attention but here in his new environs, the recently transferred LA cop found himself something of an outcast.

With a paper coffee cup in one hand, he was reading through a report on the computer when he heard his name.

He looked around.

"Hey, Kyle! Big city boy. Look alive."

Alex Rodriguez was heading over.

Kyle closed the file he was looking at and put down his coffee. "What can I do for you, Sergeant Rodriguez?"

His colleague gave him an irritated look. "It's Alex. At least it's Alex if you want to fit in around here. Anyway, I thought you might be interested in this. One of your cases came up."

Kyle smiled, pretending not to understand. "My cases, Alex?"

Alex waved his hands in circles. "The *supernatural*," he said, putting on a mock spooky voice. He cleared his throat. "I'm sorry. That's a little inappropriate. But I mean it's the kind of case you're interested in. Everyone knows you transferred here because of the rumors."

Kyle hadn't come because of the rumors. He'd come because the facts supported them. Palm Beach had become a little hotbed for rather unusual activities over the past few months and there was a chance here that he might find what he'd been looking for all these years.

Of course, he couldn't say a thing about this to Alex. At least, not yet.

With a slight shrug, he climbed to his feet. "I just came here to help, Alex. I've cracked a couple of unsolved murders back in LA. Maybe I can crack a few of the ones you've got here."

"Well, then." Alex gave him a clap on the shoulder. "Come and take a look at *this* one."

. . .

When they arrived, there were already two more patrol cars on the scene along with an ambulance. The victim was still lying where he'd been found and some police tape had been spread between the trees. However, Kyle didn't go over there straightaway. Instead, he walked across the street to where an officer was busy questioning a young man, barely in his twenties.

The witness's expression was a mixture of shock and boredom.

"But you must have seen *something* surely?" the officer insisted.

"There was no one," the witness said, sounding annoyed. "I've told you a million times."

"Sergeant," Kyle said, his tone gentle but firm.

The officer turned to him. "Yeah, Kyle?" Seeing the other's expression, he corrected himself. "I mean, Lieutenant Destri?"

"I'll take care of this. Why don't you go and help the others?"

The officer sighed. "Yes, sir."

When he was gone, Kyle turned to the young man. "My name's Kyle. Kyle Destri. What's yours?"

"Jay Evans," the man replied, sounding a little wary. Not that Kyle could blame him.

He smiled. "Are you all right?"

Jay let out a breath and shook his head. Then he nodded across the street. "That's messed up, that is."

"I know," Kyle told him. "I'm sorry you had to see that. But you did the right thing."

Jay didn't say anything.

"You want a ride home?"

"No, I'll drive," the other muttered. He looked up, puzzled. "I can go?"

Kyle nodded. "Yeah. You can go."

He watched a little longer as Jay climbed into his car and left. Since there was no mad acceleration or erratic swerving, it looked as though he'd make it home without any trouble.

Turning away, Kyle went back across the street to have a look at the crime scene.

He observed the crossed arms. The serene expression and the puncture wounds. Then he turned to a forensics expert behind him. "Anything?"

The lady shrugged before turning back to her work. "We've got some fingerprints and a DNA sample but not much else at this point."

Kyle looked at the body again. The kid was so young.

"Thanks," he murmured.

Alex came up behind him, shaking his head. "Doesn't look promising, does it?"

Kyle shrugged. "Maybe they'll find a match. Come on. Let's go back to the station."

Alex frowned. "Giving up already?"

"No," Kyle told him. "But I've seen all I need to see here."

Tuesday

Home from class, Portia slung her bag down beside the door and stopped. Lying sprawled across the sofa, her eyes hooded as though she had only just woken up, Ivana smiled at her.

"Have you been sleeping all day?" Portia asked.

Ivana stretched, even this movement languid. "Maybe. What time is it?"

"Two," Portia told her. "In the afternoon. And did you forget something? Tuesday morning? Nine o'clock? It's a core class. We *have* to attend."

Ivana sat up. "I know. I just forgot."

With a shake of her head, Portia sat beside her and grabbed the television remote.

The screen flickered to life and Portia was confronted with a momentary glimpse of a grieving woman, followed by a scene of police gathered around a cordoned off area and then a reporter.

"The community is distraught over this tragedy. That a boy, fifteen, in the prime of his life and the best of health, can simply die, his heart just ceasing to beat, makes no sense. But there's more. Who actually found this boy? And why did they leave him out in that manner without attempting to contact the authorities? These questions—"

Ivana cast her eyes down. "Turn it off, would you?"

Portia muted the TV and looked at her friend. "Are you all right?"

"I'm fine."

"You don't look fine. Is it that kid on the news?"

Ivana shook her head.

"Family stuff then? Are you upset with your mom for dumping you here or something?"

"I don't want to talk about my mother," Ivana said.

"Why?"

"I can't tell you."

Portia felt herself getting annoyed. "Can't tell me what?"

Ivana sighed. "Portia. I wish I could tell you everything. I do. But I can't. So just let it go."

Portia tried another tact. "Ivana, what's wrong? Are you and your mother in some kind of trouble? Are you hiding from something?"

Ivana shook her head. "No. We're not in trouble. It's… it's complicated. But trust me. You have *nothing* to worry about. You—" She broke off for a moment, looking embarrassed, then reached out and clasped her hands. "Look, I need you to trust me."

Portia pulled her hands free. "Trust you? I don't even know you. Look, what's come over you anyway?"

Ivana sighed in disgust and turned away. "Nothing. Forget it." She climbed to her feet and went to the kitchen, leaving Portia bewildered.

The way Ivana had held her hands and the look in her eyes... What was all that about? And why did she suddenly want Ivana to come back?

Somewhere in the room, there was a jingly tune. It took her a moment to realize it was her phone ringing in her bag.

She went and answered it. "Hey, Jay. What's up?"

Jay's voice was almost unrecognizable. "Hey, Portia. Do you think you could come over?"

There was a commotion at the police station, though not of the work related kind.

A metal bar had been braced between a door frame and, as a crowd of his fellow officers looked on, Alex Rodriguez was performing one handed pull-ups.

"F'ing, eh!" one of the guys exclaimed as Alex dropped to the floor. "Thirty in a row!"

Alex grinned at him. "Fair's fair."

The man shook his head and handed over a couple of hundred dollar bills. "Son of a bitch," he muttered, his disappointment at losing the bet mixed with admiration.

Another officer put a hand on his shoulders. "Didn't you hear, Dave? Last week, Alex singlehandedly took down two guys on PCP. Unarmed!" He laughed.

A few of the others shook Alex's hand and someone made a spirited attempt at disassembling the pull-up bar before the chief came in, though he wasn't quite fast enough.

"Hey!" a voice called out across the room and a burly looking middle-aged man came out of his office. "What are you guys doing to my station? Pack it up!"

"Already on it, Chief!"

The chief shook his head with a bemused smile and went back in his office. "I don't pay you guys to play around all day."

"I thought the taxpayers pay us, Chief Hardgrave!" someone called out.

"Stow it, Reeds!" the chief called back before he closed the door. "I know where you live!"

This got a few more laughs from the dispersing crowd.

Pocketing his prize, Alex smiled to himself and went to his desk to get out his lunch. As he ate his bread roll, he brought up the last file he'd been looking at on the computer.

He was then aware of someone standing behind him. He turned round to see Kyle.

"That was quite a show, Alex," Kyle told him. "Are you free now?"

Alex winced and waved for him to sit in a spare seat beside him. "Sorry about that. I know we've got a case. It's just... you know. Sometimes you've just got to blow off some steam. And, besides, Dave and I made that bet last week."

Kyle's face remained impassive.

Alex sighed. "Never mind. What's up, Kyle?"

"I saw the news reports today," Kyle said. "And I want to know something. Did they doctor the reports the last time this type of thing happened?"

Alex took another bite of his bread roll, intent on finishing it. "What are you talking about?"

"Did they lie about the cause of death?"

"The heart failure?" Alex asked, frowning. "You think the media should be telling everyone we found two puncture wounds and a body drained of blood?"

Kyle smiled. "Not at all. Obviously, no one wants to cause a mass panic. I understand that. No, I'm just trying to get an idea of the complete picture. Knowing how previous incidents like this were reported might be useful."

Alex shrugged. "I don't remember. We liaised with the media a little on these types of cases. Sometimes they went with heart troubles. Sometimes a stroke. But, as I said, I can't remember them all. And, besides, I can't see the relevance."

"It *might* be helpful."

Alex studied his new partner carefully. "So tell me, Kyle... You said you were trying to put together the picture. How much of the picture do you have? Last night, you didn't even look at the forensics report."

Kyle paused before answering. "A little over six months ago, there were three unusual killings over a handful of days. They were similar to the one last night, with one key difference. The wounds were more jagged and the victims were just left sprawled on the ground. So this is a different perpetrator for starters."

"*Oh*," Alex said with an exaggerated nod. "Well, I guess we can close the book on that one then. A killer can't change their style, right?"

"The first of those killings occurred not long after a new resident moved into the area," Kyle continued, ignoring the remark. "And there hasn't been another one since he disappeared."

This succeeded in shutting Alex up.

"You're sure of that?" he asked, once he found his voice again. "I mean, there must be a lot of people coming and going from this town. You really think you can pin those killings on one guy? And you think he's no longer with us?"

"That's what I'm saying, Alex. And, sure, there have been a lot of people coming and going. Visitors. Permanent residents. But he's the one who best fits the facts. His time of arrival is pretty close to the first of the murders and his disappearance follows pretty close on the heels of the last one. And what's more, he didn't move out of his home. All his things were still there. He still had rent owed and other things. But he just went off the grid entirely. And there have been several other situations like that one, with enough differences in the forensic reports to suggest different people were involved each time."

Alex frowned, his bread roll now forgotten.

"Do you think I could have a look at your findings later?" he asked. "In more detail?"

"Of course," Kyle said. "I'd be glad to have some help. As I said, I'm trying to figure this thing out."

When Portia got to Jay's place, he was on the sofa too. She heard him call her to come in. Pushing open the unlocked door, she was startled by her friend's change of appearance. Unlike Ivana, who just looked as though she'd been sleeping in, Jay looked exhausted. And more than a little unwell.

Portia rushed to his side in case he fell on the floor. "What happened?"

Jay leaned his head back, closed his eyes and sighed. "Did you see the news? About that kid who was found dead on the sidewalk last night?"

Portia watched her friend in trepidation. "You found him?"

Jay nodded, his eyes still closed. "And his heart hadn't just stopped. Someone had drained the blood out of his body. And there were two puncture wounds on his neck. Now, I'm a level headed kind of guy and I'm not prone to wild flights of fancy but... I've heard other guys talking about this place. I think you know what I mean. People don't like to talk about it much but there are things out there that we don't learn about in high school biology, aren't there?"

Portia frowned. Jay sounded pretty sure of what he'd seen. "I suppose there's a lot we don't know about the world we live in," she conceded. "And there are probably a few things we can't account for even in the twenty-first century."

Jay heaved a sigh. "But we *can* account for them. Bite marks. Drained blood. We're not like Victorian era characters stumbling in the dark and waiting for someone to turn on the light. We've read all those stories and we've seen all those movies and TV shows. We've got the folklore going back centuries. Well, what if some of that stuff is on the mark?"

Portia sighed. "I don't know, Jay. I'm sure there's a perfectly—"

"Logical explanation?" Jay asked, looking up. "Was that what you were going to say? Like in every vampire story ever?"

Portia took a moment to think up a reply. "A perfectly *natural cause* was what I was going to say." She shook her head and climbed to her feet. "Look, do you want something to drink? Coffee?" She shook her head. "No, something soothing. Tea?"

Jay sighed. "Wish I had some. But coffee sounds good."

Portia went into his kitchen. "Hey," she called out as she boiled a pot. "Have you had anything to eat today?"

"Not hungry." Jay's voice was a flat monotone.

"Well, you've got to eat something," Portia said, looking around and opening various cupboards.

"I'll be all right," Jay said. "You don't have to stay here all day."

"I'll stay here all night if I have to," Portia told him. She pulled out a bag of a chips and looked at him. "You're my friend."

Two blocks away, Liz pulled up across the street from the scene of last night's crime. The police had already cleared the area. There was no tape cordoning off the area. No morbid chalk outline on the pavement. Nothing to remind anyone of the terrible tragedy that had occurred there.

But there was an unsettling silence in the street. Nobody was outside and the occasional leaf blowing in the breeze sounded unnaturally loud.

Liz climbed out of her car and walked over to where the kid had been found, crouched down and placed a wreath of flowers on the sidewalk.

For a minute, she stayed there in silence. Then she took a breath, wiped away a few small tears and stood up.

The afternoon was getting late, she saw, and the summer's day had somehow taken on a winter's aesthetic.

She looked at the roofs of the houses around her and then the trees, thinking of how the predator may have taken its prey. But she immediately knew this wasn't the way to be looking at it. The boy had appeared serene in death, smiling. He wasn't taken by surprise. He'd gone, Liz realized, willingly into the arms of his killer.

And she doubted he'd done so right here at the site where he'd been found. In fact, she began to doubt he'd been killed here at all.

A teenage boy, she thought. Walking hand in hand with a beautiful girl he'd met. At a cafe? Just walking down the street? And where would they go?

An image came to mind of a park bench, up on the town's small bluff overlooking the ocean. There were several, she knew. Spread out enough for people to have their own quiet little space. This made sense.

She checked that no cars were coming and crossed the street to her own.

As she drove off, Kyle Destri—who'd been sitting in his own car a hundred yards back—watched her go. Frowning, he got out and walked down to the scene of the crime. He found the wreath Liz had left then he jogged back to his car and followed after her.

The afternoon sun was falling toward the ocean horizon as Liz pulled into the parking lot on the bluff. She got out of the vehicle and took a moment to savor the sea breeze. She'd always loved the ocean, as far back as she could remember. And she could remember a fair way.

She looked to either side of her. There were a handful of people out and about. Some couples. A family packing up their car, ready to leave. A dark handsome man sitting behind the wheel of another car, trying not to look as though he were watching her.

Liz pretended not to notice. He wasn't the person she was looking for, but she wondered what he was up to. He'd pulled into the parking lot right behind her and if he'd followed her from the crime scene...

She shook her head. That was it. This was some cop who'd seen her there and jumped straight to the wrong conclusion.

She wasn't worried about being implicated in the crime—she could clear her name without too much trouble if the investigation came her way—but it did make things difficult.

However, as she noticed another newcomer out on the bluff, she put the thought aside. It was Ivana, the young woman who'd joined her Monday morning lecture.

Ivana surveyed the area as Liz had and when at last her eyes came to rest on her, they widened for a moment in either surprise or alarm. Then, with a slight scowl, she turned away.

Liz threw a glance toward the sun then jogged after her.

"Ivana?"

She stopped and turned round, with a sweet smile playing on her lips. "Liz. Hi."

"Hi, Ivana. I was just wondering how you're doing. Have you finalized your enrolment for the semester? Found a place to stay and all that?"

Ivana's smile remained but her expression was otherwise blank. "Yes to the second question. Not yet to the first. Was there anything else?"

What are you doing here? That was the burning question Liz wanted to ask. That and where was she staying.

However, right then, Liz was also struck by the realization that Ivana seemed wary of her. She already knew what Ivana was but was it also possible that Ivana knew what *she* was?

"No," she said, answering the question. "I just wanted to check on you. That's all."

Ivana nodded. "Okay. Well, it was good to see you, Liz."

"You too, Ivana. Take care."

Liz watched as the woman walked away and breathed a sigh of relief. The sun was now dangerously close to the horizon.

Alex looked up from his desk as Kyle came into the office. "Where have *you* been?"

"I was having another look at the crime scene," Kyle replied, wandering over. "Any more leads?"

Alex shook his head and looked up at his partner. "I thought you said there was nothing more to see at that place."

"I did. But sometimes killers revisit crime scenes."

Alex took a sip of coffee. "So you're the killer then?"

"That's pretty funny, Alex." Kyle pulled out his phone and showed Alex a picture of an attractive dark-haired woman. "Any idea who this is? I know it's a long shot but—"

Alex held the phone and smiled. "Mm. She's cute. Actually, I have seen her before. She's an English lady. Works at the local college."

"Do you know her name?"

"Um, I think it's Jane or something. Or Annie? Maybe Jane."

"So... no in other words." Kyle took the phone, flicked to the next photo and passed it back to Alex. "But it gives me a place to start at least. Now any idea who this girl she's talking to is?"

Alex frowned and passed the phone back to him. "She's not talking to anyone."

"Hang on," Kyle muttered, furrowing his brow. "There was someone right there. She was..." He flicked through some more photos. "What the hell? She was talking to a girl. She was *right there*."

Alex shrugged. "Maybe you didn't press the button properly at the right time. Or there's something wrong with your phone. I wouldn't overthink it."

"Yeah," Kyle muttered, turning away but still gazing at the phone.

"Happy to help!" Alex called after him.

Not that Kyle appeared to be listening.

Wednesday

"IVANA?" PORTIA CALLED OUT.

There was no reply.

She shook her head. Surely her new friend couldn't be sleeping in. After all, *she'd* just spent the night looking after Jay and she was awake. Well, half awake at least.

"Ivana?" she tried again, stifling a yawn as she closed the front door and put her bag down.

Again, there was no reply.

Frowning, Portia opened the door to the spare room Ivana was using. She *was* asleep. Unbelievable.

It was also odd how little stuff she had. There was a light suitcase, unpacked, a bit of make–up on a shelf that Ivana was using as a dressing table, a few changes of clothes and that was it.

With a sigh, Portia decided to look on the bright side. If Ivana was going to sleep through the better part of the day, maybe she could catch up on some sleep of her own.

With lethargic movements, she made her way back to the sofa, sat down and rubbed her temples. She felt exhausted, although she knew it couldn't have all been down to looking after Jay. She'd had nights with little sleep in the past so it was hardly the first time. This level of fatigue, an exhaustion beyond exhaustion, was something else.

She lay on the sofa and closed her eyes. She hoped she wasn't coming down with something.

She was woken in the afternoon by Ivana, sitting on the arm of the sofa.

She blinked her eyes and yawned. "Hey," she said, managing a smile. "What's up?"

Ivana smiled back. "I was just watching you sleep the afternoon away."

"Yeah," Portia muttered, sitting up. "Well, I was looking after a friend all night so I've got an excuse. Why were *you* sleeping in so late?"

"I was out too."

Portia frowned. "Where?"

"Why?" Ivana asked. "Does it matter?"

Yes, it mattered. But Portia couldn't explain why. Not even to herself.

Ivana looked at her in concern. "Portia, what's bothering you?"

"I feel like you're keeping things from me," Portia said. "Like that stuff with your mother, for instance. And now you won't even answer a simple question."

When Ivana didn't reply, Portia shook her head. She was annoyed and, for reasons she couldn't grasp, saddened by her friend's reticence. "Fine. See if I care."

Ivana reached over and put a hand on hers. "No. Look, Portia. I'm sorry. I understand where you're coming from. And I *want* to tell you everything. I do. But I can't. At least not yet. You know that."

With an effort, Portia fought past her overwhelming fatigue and pushed herself to her feet. She shot her friend another irritated look and turned away. "Forget it."

Ivana reached out again. "No, Portia—wait."

Portia whirled around. "What?"

Ivana hesitated before replying, then looked over at the guitar. "I was wondering... Maybe you could play one of your songs."

Portia felt like she was lost at sea now. Where had *this* come from? "Are you kidding?"

"No, I'm serious," Ivana insisted with an honest gaze. "I want to hear you play. Please?"

Portia sighed and, oddly, she felt some of her frustration drain away. "All right."

She picked up the guitar then pulled a kitchen stool into the middle of the room and sat down. She lifted her hand, preparing to strum a chord...

"Wait," Ivana interrupted again. "When you look my way. I want to hear that one."

Portia glanced at her friend in puzzlement. *When you look my way.* That had been one of her high school compositions. She felt nothing at all now for the guy she'd written it for—in fact, she could barely remember him—and now she found the whole song rather corny.

"What makes you think you'd like it?" she asked.

"The lyrics are sweet."

Portia shrugged. "Oh well. I'm glad one of us thinks so."

She started strumming the chord progression and, at first, it sounded a little rusty as a result of having not played the song in so long. However, her fingers still remembered even if she didn't and soon, she found the right rhythm and then her voice. And as she played, she started to feel the emotions she'd felt when she'd written it two or three years before. It felt like she was singing it from the heart and the words were just a natural outpouring for the feelings she had inside.

Ivana watched her with an expression of love and admiration. And Portia felt something stirring in her as she looked back at her friend. But as she finished playing, the feeling faded.

Ivana, for her part though, was beaming. "That was incredible, Portia."

Portia forced a smile and got up. "Thanks." She put the guitar back.

Ivana frowned. "You won't play another one?"

Portia sighed again. "Isn't one enough?" Then she shook her head. What was Ivana doing? And what was *she* doing? "No, no. Ivana, it's not the right time. I'm worried about Jay."

"Jay?"

"My friend. He—" She broke off. Letting Ivana into her life was one thing but letting her into Jay's was another.

"He's a guy I hang out with at college and he's just had a pretty rough experience."

"Do you want to talk about it?" Ivana asked, looking concerned.

"I'd rather not, Ivana. Just let it go, okay? I need some time alone."

Ivana got up and patted her on the shoulder. "All right. Maybe you should get some rest. I might have an afternoon nap as well."

"But you slept all morning," Portia told her.

Ivana glanced over her shoulder as she went to her room. "Maybe I'm just not a hundred percent today." She turned away.

"Maybe something's going round," Portia muttered to herself. She began to feel a bit woozy and her earlier lethargy was creeping back. Perhaps a rest would do her some good.

As the early afternoon sun flooded through her office window, Liz was arranging her lecture notes for the next class.

There was a quiet knock on the door.

Opening it, she saw a rather handsome dark man. Well-dressed in smart casual attire with a familiar face. It took a moment for Liz to place him as she hadn't met him before. But she had *seen* him before.

"Hello, can I help you?" she asked, resisting the impulse to add 'officer' to the end of the question since he hadn't identified himself as one yet.

"Are you Liz Garnier?" the man asked in return, his voice pleasant and his tone polite.

"That's me," Liz replied with a smile.

"I'm Lieutenant Destri from the Palm Beach police," the man introduced himself, holding up his badge. "I wonder if I could ask you a few questions. It might assist me in an important investigation."

Liz gestured for him to come in. "Of course."

She closed the door behind him, waved him to a seat then sat across from him. "What would you like to ask me about?"

"Last night," the man said, "I saw you at the bluff talking to a young woman. It would have been around five-forty. Do you remember who were talking to? I got the impression you know her. At least a little bit."

Liz's smile remained. "She's a student. Well, a *prospective* student anyway. She came to one of my classes once and I asked if she'd finalized her enrolment yet."

"And had she?"

"Not yet."

And she wasn't going to, Liz knew. Enrolling would require paperwork. Identification. Photos.

Besides, she was fairly certain her 'prospective student' had already got what she wanted from her studies at Palm Beach College.

"Would the college administration have any more information on her?"

Liz shrugged. "They might."

The man smiled and climbed to his feet. "Well, I'll give them a try. Do you remember this girl's name?"

Liz got up as well, and picked up a scrap of paper and a pen. "Ivana. Ivana Kovac."

She wrote the name down and handed it to the man.

"Thank you, Miss Garnier," the man said, folding the paper and putting it in his trouser pocket. "I appreciate you giving me your time."

"No trouble at all."

The man passed her a card. "Here. If you remember anything else, give me a call."

Liz looked at the card. Lieutenant Kyle Destri.

"Sure," she said, turning her gaze back to him and feeling a pang of sympathy. The young man was a picture of reassuring strength but if he got too close in his investigation, Ivana could snap him in two. And there was nothing she could say to warn him.

The lieutenant frowned. "Miss Garnier? Is there something wrong?"

Liz smiled and shook her head.

And, abruptly, the man's manner changed. All traces of formality were gone. "This girl... Ivana. She's not like other girls, is she, Liz?"

Liz hesitated, wondering if she should say something, but stayed silent.

The lieutenant's features changed into a warm smile. "You don't trust me yet. I understand. But I'll tell you what. I'm going to take a chance and put my mad little theory out there. Maybe you'll think I'm crazy. But, as I said, I'm going to take the chance.

"I saw you at a crime scene yesterday. You studied it. Not like a perpetrator returning to look for anything they left behind... or one of the sick ones who goes back to admire their handiwork. You studied it like a detective would. And then you went to the bluff looking for that girl. You *knew* she was the one who did the deed."

Liz said nothing.

"But not because you knew she'd been there the night before or because she knew the victim. Or anything else you might call conventional evidence. You knew she was the perpetrator because of the nature of the crime. You knew she was the only *thing* in town that was capable of doing something like that. Draining someone's blood from their veins. Drinking them dry."

"A vampire," he added when Liz didn't take the bait. "Am I right?"

Liz smiled and shook her head. "I'm sorry, Lieutenant. It's an interesting theory but I'm afraid I don't know anything about vampires. Except in stories."

When she saw the earnest look in the detective's eyes, she felt bad about lying to him but she couldn't be sure he wasn't trying to trap her somehow. Although if it *was* all an act, it was a hell of a performance.

"Well, as I said," the detective told her, "if you think of anything else, give me a call." He gave her a curt nod. "Thank you again for your time, Miss Garnier."

Liz put a little more warmth in her smile. "Please. Call me Liz."

"Then by the same token," the man replied, returning the smile, "you can call me Kyle." He opened the door, took a step through and stopped. "By the way, I took some photos when you were talking to this girl. Ivana.

And you know what? She didn't show up in any of them." He gave her a knowing look. "Curious, isn't it?"

Once the detective—Kyle—had left, Liz's smile disappeared. She wondered if she should have played that differently. She *had* contemplated giving the man another name beside Ivana's. Or just pretending she didn't know the name at all. But if the man had found *her*, then he might well have known Ivana's name already. And getting caught in a lie by a police officer on a murder investigation wouldn't be a smart move.

No, she decided. She couldn't have done anything else.

But the fact remained that the luxury of time had just been taken from her. If Kyle Destri found Ivana Kovac before she did, he was a dead man.

And as she looked at the pile of lecture notes and folders on her desk, she wondered if she even had time for her last lecture today.

Then the door swung open and Natasha looked in with a little grin. "Hey, Liz. Aren't you going to class?"

Suppressing a sigh, Liz put her smile back in place.

With no ready-made excuse at hand, she guessed she had no choice in the matter.

• • •

Kyle had known more than a few cops over the years who struggled with the concept of the stakeout. They'd grumble. They'd binge eat. Or they'd alternate between the two.

Kyle however just let his mind and body relax, sliding into an almost meditative state. Also, he'd had the presence of mind to check when Liz's lecture ended so he didn't have to wait around in the car *that* long.

As he sat with the window down, he emptied his mind and tried not to think of anything. Liz. The boy who'd died. The case. It was amazing how therapeutic it was to just switch off every now and then. And waiting for Liz to come out was a perfect time to do it.

Besides, he had a feeling that he might need to save his energy for later on.

Inside the college gates, Liz had finished her lecture. And she'd done such a great job acting like nothing was wrong that she'd almost fooled herself. But now the class was finished, the dread was settling in again.

Then a horrible thought struck her. She put her notes and folders on her desk—she could find the proper homes for them later—and picked up the phone.

"Hello?" The voice was her daughter's. Liz was startled by how drained she sounded.

"Portia, it's me."

"Oh." Portia said, the simple utterance so flat it was as though she'd just come out of a coma. "Hi, Mom."

"Are you all right? Portia?"

"I'm fine, Mom."

Liz frowned. "You don't sound fine to me. Do you want me to come over?"

"No, no. I'm fine. I'm just a little tired. Just had a late night. That's all."

"Why?"

"I had to go to Jay's place. Jay—" There was an audible sob and Portia broke off.

"Portia? What's wrong?"

"Jay found that kid the other night," her daughter replied, her voice unsteady and filled with emotion. "The one in the news."

Liz took a deep breath and sat down. "Portia... I'm sorry. How is he?"

"Not good."

Liz held her head in her hand and covered her eyes. She'd known what Ivana was the moment she'd come into her class, and what she was capable of. But she'd made the mistake of thinking she had the situation in control. She'd been too complacent since she'd brought Portia here. And she'd been overconfident. Yes, there'd been an incident six months ago in which three people had died. But that had been different. *Ivana* was different.

For one thing, she hadn't counted on her taking a life so soon. Nor had she counted on her own daughter being dragged into all of this. And she should have picked up on it sooner. She'd seen Matt sitting in the cafeteria a few hours earlier all alone. No Portia. No Jay. She should have realized something was up.

"Mom? Are you there?"

And now, it seemed, she'd lost track of external time as well.

"I'm here, Portia," she said. "I'm coming over."

"You don't need to come over, Mom. I told you. I'm fine."

Liz frowned. "Portia. I've got to ask you something. Do you remember Ivana Kovac? That Czech student from class the other day?"

There was a noticeable hesitation. "Um... yes. What about her?"

"Do you know where she's staying, by any chance? Do any of you have her number or know where she is? Maybe Jay or Matt?"

"No."

Liz braced herself. There was one last thing she could try but she didn't want to do it.

"Portia. Is she staying with you?"

There was another pause.

"No." There was an audible strain in her daughter's voice when she replied.

"Portia?"

This time, her daughter couldn't answer at all.

Liz's heart thudded hard in her chest and she felt beads of cold sweat on her forehead.

"I'm coming over," she said. And hung up.

With tears in her eyes, Portia lowered her phone. Ivana had emerged from her bedroom, watching her with an almost unreadable expression.

What are you? Portia wanted to ask.

The question rose unbidden as though from the depths of her soul. But it hadn't risen from nothing. Try as she might, Portia had been unable to tell her mother the truth just before and it seemed as clear as the waters of a glacial lake that it was Ivana who'd stopped her.

"I'm going to have a little walk outside," her flat mate said, smiling before she stepped through the door. "Stay here."

Portia grimaced as the door closed. Frozen on the sofa as if held back by invisible bonds, she didn't feel as though she had a choice.

Then, as if her unseen bonds snapped from too much tension, she fell forward. And for a few brief moments, she knew, she was free.

. . .

On another sofa in another unit, Jay watched as a series of FBI warnings scrolled down his screen. In a futile gesture, he held down the 'menu' button on the DVD remote. As expected, it had no effect. However, somehow it didn't bother him today. Reading through the laundry list of penalties for movie piracy was better than remembering that kid from two nights ago.

God, he would have had a father and a mother, wouldn't he? What were they going through right now?

Tears slid down his cheeks as the menu appeared on the TV and he couldn't bring himself to play the movie. For a few moments, he just stared at the screen.

Then his phone rang.

"Hello," he answered, his voice hollow in his ears.

"Jay. It's me. It's Portia."

Jay sat up and turned the TV off. Portia sounded even more upset than *he* did.

"Are you all right?" he asked.

There was an audible sob. "Jay. I'm in trouble."

"What's going on?"

A moment passed before Portia answered. "I—I can't say."

"What do you mean, you can't say?"

"I can't. I want to and I can't! Can't you come round? Please? I need you to get me *out* of here."

. . .

As she hung up, Portia knew she wasn't alone. She hadn't heard Ivana open the door or seen her come back inside but she knew she was there.

With a lump in her throat and her heart thudding, she lifted her head to see her standing in front of her with enough metaphorical fire in her eyes to incinerate her.

"Who were you talking to?"

"No one," Portia stammered. "Just—a friend. Jay. From class."

Ivana lunged, grabbed her hair and yanked her head back. Portia gasped, her eyes widening in terror, but she couldn't speak. Or move. And sensing the raw strength in Ivana's grip, she doubted it would make much difference if she could.

Tears slid down her cheeks. She was going to die. It didn't matter now whether Jay made it or not. All she could hope for now was that Ivana would make it quick.

However, the sweet release she was anticipating took another form as Ivana relaxed her grip and smiled.

She caressed Portia's cheeks and brushed her tears away. "It's all right," she murmured. "He won't interfere with us."

Portia didn't know whether to feel relieved or more terrified. But as Ivana sat beside her and stroked her hair, she felt a sense of tranquility. Now, it seemed, everything was all right.

"Just relax," Ivana told her.

Portia nodded and closed her eyes.

When Liz reached her car, the sun had almost set. She climbed in, started it up and took off. Wondering what she'd find when she reached her daughter and imagining all kinds of terrible possibilities, she didn't notice the unmarked car that took off after her as she left the college parking lot.

It took Jay a little over a minute to drive round to Portia's street. He drove the length of it, checking the numbers of the houses and apartments on either side. He'd seen the place before but there were a few similar buildings around it. He slowed down as he came to the 440s and then he saw it. 453 and the light was on in Unit 3.

From the street, there was no way he could tell if Portia was alone. And if that creature who'd murdered that kid was inside...

"Fuck it," he muttered as he turned off the engine and got out. "What's the worst that can happen? Apart from getting myself killed."

He jogged across the lawn and knocked on the door. When there was no answer, he tried to open it.

It was unlocked.

"Portia!" he shouted as he stepped inside. "It's me! Jay!" Then, catching the scene on the sofa in front of him, he immediately regretted making so much noise.

Portia was in an almost trance–like state, small rivulets of blood trickling down her neck from two small puncture wounds, lying in the arms of the new girl he'd seen in class the day before yesterday. Ivana.

For a moment he was held in awe. Fascinated by how little like a monster the vampire appeared. Her mouth was drawn back by only the slightest of margins and her incisors seemed more prominent—were they all a vampire's fangs were?—but there were no other signs that this creature was anything other than human.

These thoughts passed through his mind in an instant, replaced by the more pressing observation that Ivana was glaring at him.

She lay Portia down on the sofa, lovingly it seemed, and climbed to her feet. Her incisors receded but she didn't look any less dangerous.

"Who the hell do you think you are?" she demanded, walking toward Jay with her shoulders hunched forward. "Interrupting me in *this* moment. Of all the moments you could come in uninvited..."

On the sofa, Portia opened her eyes and looked around in a daze.

"I've been waiting for this moment for months," Ivana continued, heedless of Portia's movements—though the victim of her predations was now pushing herself off the sofa.

Ivana stretched out one hand, gripped Jay by the throat and hoisted him a foot off the ground. Without any apparent effort, she marched across the room and slammed him against the wall. Using both hands, Jay tried to no avail to pry her fingers from his throat as she crushed his windpipe.

"You pathetic little man," Ivana said, her voice almost at a whisper.

"Ivana!"

Ivana whirled about at Portia's cry.

"If you want me," Portia said, "then let him go."

"I will have you whether you want it or not," Ivana told her, paying no attention to Jay's attempts to pry himself from her grip.

"But..." Portia hesitated. She was terrified but she knew if she did nothing, Ivana would strangle the life out of Jay. "Wouldn't you rather I come with you… willingly?"

Not loosening her grip, Ivana lowered Jay. Although her gaze remained on Portia. "You would do that?"

"If you let my friend go."

Ivana turned to Jay then back to Portia. "But I will not have him with us when I turn you. We must be alone."

"We will be," Portia said, stepping closer. Trying to still her emotions, she looked at Jay. "Did you come by car?"

Jay tried to break free of Ivana's grip one more time and Ivana shook him, making him abandon the effort. Unable to speak, and with pain and betrayal in his eyes, he nodded.

Portia extended her hand. "Give me the keys, Jay."

With obvious reluctance, Jay did so and then Ivana flung him to the floor. As he gasped for breath, Ivana took the keys from Portia. "Come."

Portia followed, giving Jay an imploring look over her shoulder. "I'm sorry," she murmured but Jay, still lying immobile on the floor, just grimaced.

Outside, she climbed into Jay's car, with Ivana in the driver's seat. Saying nothing, Ivana started the engine. Portia swallowed, glancing at her companion as they pulled away from the curb, and braced herself for what she had to do.

It was a risk of course. She knew that. A little superstition perpetuated in books and movies that could be total bullshit for all she knew. But she remembered Ivana hesitating outside her place the other day, waiting to be invited in. Maybe there was some truth in the stories.

Portia rested her palm on the door handle, got ready—

And with a squeal of tires, another car roared past and came to a screeching halt across the street in front of them.

Ivana slammed the brakes, bringing them to a sudden halt of their own… and Portia threw open the door and ran.

A second car stopped behind Ivana as well, Portia noticed. Someone in the wrong place at the wrong time. But she knew there was no time to warn them. Having seen Ivana throw Jay around like a rag doll, she didn't fancy her chances if she caught her.

Without slowing, she scooped up a loose stone and threw it at the sliding glass door of a nearby house. It didn't shatter it but it made a good sized hole, which she ran for. Then turning her shoulder to the glass, she crashed through, landing in the house on the floor. She ignored the wailing burglar alarm she'd set off, along with the cries of alarmed neighbors and the pain from numerous small cuts, as there was only one thing she could think of right then.

Catching her breath and turning back, she saw how close Ivana had been behind her. However, she was no longer coming any closer. The vampire was pacing just outside but it seemed an invisible barrier prevented her from passing the point where the sliding door had been.

Portia took a breath in relief. Her gamble had paid off and the only thing that remained to be seen—apart from how much trouble she'd be in when the owners or the cops turned up—was what the vampire would do next.

Or, Portia just realized, not...

From the car behind Jay's, a man had hopped out and was approaching Ivana, drawing a gun. "Ma'am! Step away from the window and put your hands up!"

Portia looked on horrified as Ivana turned her hellish glare on the newcomer. But as she did, there was another surprise. There was someone else out there as well now, most likely the driver of the car that had cut Ivana off just moments before. Crouching in the middle of the street and holding what could only be a crossbow.

It was her mother.

"Watch out, Kyle!" Liz shouted.

Her new acquaintance turned in surprise, his back to Ivana. But for the moment, he was out of the way.

Though a moment was now all that Liz had.

Grimacing, knowing that what happened now would change her life forever, Liz took aim and fired.

Ivana, for her part, had just enough time to see where the wooden arrow came from before it pierced her through the chest. With a muffled cry of anguish, she fell to her knees and turned to Portia. And where there had been fire in her eyes, there was now only sorrow.

Small tears slid down her cheeks as her gaze darkened, then she keeled over and lay on the grass.

Portia felt an overwhelming desire to go to her but a second later, the body crumpled as though several centuries were now taking their toll. And as Ivana returned to the ash from which she had sprung, it blew away into nothingness.

Portia knew she should have felt relieved. Instead, with her terror now forgotten, she felt a sudden overwhelming sense of grief. And burying her face in her hands, she fell to her knees and wept.

On the street, Liz rose to her feet and lowered the crossbow.

"It's lucky you had that thing," a voice said at her side.

For a moment, she didn't register it. Then, coming out of her shock, she turned to see Kyle beside her.

"Look," he said. "I'll go and see if that girl's all right. You go and—"

Liz handed him the crossbow, stopping him mid-sentence.

"Put this in my car, will you?" she asked in a murmur, almost inaudible over the alarm and the noise of people coming out of their homes.

Kyle frowned. "In a minute, everyone in this neighborhood's—"

Liz nodded in Portia's direction. "That's my daughter. And she needs me."

Leaving Kyle cradling the crossbow, she ran to Portia and put her arms around her.

Kyle in the meantime noticed a young man—shaky on his feet—who was also watching the scene unfold. Recognition, as it usually did for him, kicked in straightaway. It was the same young man who'd found the kid the other night. Jay.

He wondered what his connection was to tonight's events. There were a million questions he wanted to ask him. A million questions he wanted to ask Liz. But now, he knew, was not the time.

He jogged to Liz's car, stashed the crossbow in the trunk before anyone could see it and parked the car on the side of the road. As he took the keys from the ignition, he noticed Jay moving the car Ivana had been driving. For a moment, this had Kyle perplexed but then he remembered from the other night that the car belonged to him.

Maybe Jay had been looking for Ivana as well, or maybe he was friends with the girl Ivana had been chasing. That seemed more likely. But Liz could fill him in on what really happened here later. After tonight, she might be more willing to let him in.

Jay had now parked his car behind Liz's and seemed at a loss as to what to do next. Kyle decided to walk over and help him in this decision. He leant by the driver's window. "Hey, son. Remember me?"

Jay nodded. "Yeah."

"That's right. It's me. Kyle. Look, I've got to get your friend and her mother somewhere safe. And calm things down here."

"What about Portia?" Jay asked.

Kyle guessed this was Liz's daughter. "She'll be all right. She's not in trouble."

This seemed to be enough and Jay acquiesced fairly readily. Once he was gone, Kyle moved his own car and after that, it was time to move the onlookers back.

"It's all right," he told the neighbors.

"She broke into that guy's house!" someone in the crowd called, pointing at Portia.

"She didn't break in," Kyle said, adopting a soothing voice that always served him well in situations like this.

"Someone pushed her through the door. I saw the whole thing."

"Who pushed her?"

"I don't know but I'll find out." Kyle raised his hands, palms outward. "Now, if you can all return to your homes, I need to call the alarm company and the owner of this house."

As the crowd dispersed, he stepped over the broken glass and retrieved the stone Portia had thrown at the door. He put it in his pocket and walked up to Liz, who was still holding Portia.

"Liz," he said. "You'd better get out of here before my colleagues arrive."

With a nod, Liz climbed to her feet, helping her daughter up as well. "Come on, Portia."

The girl seemed a bit more composed now, although it was likely she was too tired to cry any more. Kyle was startled by how drained she appeared.

"Thank you, Kyle," Liz told him as she helped her daughter across the lawn. She stopped for a moment to pick up a slender wooden item lying in the grass and then walked with Portia to her car.

When she reached it and she and Portia both climbed in, the wailing of the burglar alarm stopped. It was amazing how quiet everything seemed afterward.

Liz turned the key in the ignition. "All right, honey. You're staying with me tonight. I don't want you home alone for a while until you're okay."

As they pulled away from the curb, Portia turned to her. "You knew."

Liz kept her eyes on the road, saying nothing.

"You knew," Portia repeated. "And you didn't tell me."

Liz opened the door and stepped inside, Portia leaning on her shoulder. She flicked on the living room light— flinching from the sudden brightness—and helped her daughter into an adjacent room where her old bed waited. Unmade but, with a light blanket at the end and a firm pillow, it was just what Portia needed.

"I'll get you a glass of water," Liz told her. "And then you need to sleep."

"Mom?" Portia murmured as she started to turn away.

"Yes?"

"Can you call Jay and let him know I'm all right?"

Liz gave her daughter a smile in the dim secondhand light coming in from the next room. "It's next on my to-do list."

"Do it now. I want to talk."

Liz sighed. "We'll talk later, honey. Right now, you need rest. Lots of it."

Portia sat up and hit the pillow. "I don't want to sleep! I was almost killed by a vampire, forced to break into someone's home to protect myself, and I saw *my own mother* murder someone right in front of my eyes. And..." She broke off with a sob. "And I miss Ivana. I know, she tried to kill me. She hurt Jay and she killed that kid the other night. But I miss her. I..."

Liz nodded, her gaze filled with pity. "You felt something for her. I know. The feeling was real." She sat at the end of the bed. "And there was a reason for it. You see, Ivana wasn't trying to kill you. She was trying to turn you."

"I know that," Portia replied, quieter now. For a moment, her fatigue had overpowered her emotion. "Of course I know it. But turning me's the same thing, isn't it? I'd be *undead*."

Liz managed a smile. "Things are either dead or alive, honey. They can't be both. And vampires are as alive as you or me." The smile faded. "But you would have changed."

"And turned into a monster like her?"

"I don't know," Liz admitted. "Not everyone turns out like Ivana. Some aren't as bad. Some are a whole lot worse. Some manage to stay true to themselves, while others lose themselves entirely. But none of them can make their own blood and so they need the blood of others to survive. And that's not an easy thing to live with."

Portia frowned. "You pity them."

"I do. And I pitied Ivana. I didn't take any pleasure in what I had to do."

"But you didn't hesitate." There was a note of accusation in Portia's voice. "You had that crossbow — which I've *never* seen before—and you shot her. The woman who raised me could never have done something like that. Tonight, you were like a total stranger."

Liz looked for the right words but couldn't find them. The moment she'd feared with Portia had arrived, and much sooner than she'd expected. Although, now she wondered if a few more years would make that much difference. How could she ever be ready for this moment?

"All right," she said. "You want to know the truth about me. That's fair. After everything that's happened these past few days, you deserve some answers. And I can't keep things hidden from you forever. We're family."

"But when were you going to tell me?"

Though her voice remained steady, Liz's eyes welled up. "When would the right time be? How could I even bring it up? All your life, as far as you've been concerned, vampires have been make believe. How on Earth was I going to tell you they were real?"

"But you knew about Ivana," Portia told her. "And you didn't warn me."

"I'm sorry you had to go through all that," Liz said, reaching out her hand to brush a tear from Portia's cheek. "You know that."

Portia pushed her away with an irritated gesture.

Liz sat still a moment, not knowing what to say. It was clear her daughter would need some time to work her way through everything. Possibly quite a lot of it.

"I thought I could deal with Ivana without putting you in danger," she told her. "I've done it before. It's not the first time we've had a vampire in the neighborhood. It's not even the first time since we moved here. But I didn't know Ivana was staying with you and that she had you under her influence. If I had, I would have stopped her much sooner."

She was met with a stony silence almost as hard as her daughter's gaze.

"I'm sorry things got as far as they did," she tried.

"You already said you're sorry," Portia told her. "I don't want sorries. I want answers. Like, who are you?"

Liz's gaze though remained compassionate. "I've been a lot of people over a lot of years. And in that sense, there are several truths about me. But before I tell you anything about the truths you don't know, I want you to remember one you do. That no matter what, I am—and always will be—your mother. And I love you more than anyone I've ever known."

Portia nodded, her gaze softening a little. "I know."

"Good. Then I guess I can tell you some of the other truths. You know me as your mother and a professor in English literature. And I'm both. But before I was either of those, I was a guardian."

Portia watched her like Patience on a monument. And Liz knew she would go on watching until she finished her story.

"I know," she said. "That just raises another question." It looked like she'd be filling in the silences for the next little while. "But since you already know about vampires, this shouldn't be hard to explain. A guardian is a type of protector. Someone to hold the vampires back."

"Are there more of you?"

Liz knew she should have expected this question but, even so, it threw her. "What?"

Portia frowned. "Are there more of you?"

Liz drew a breath and let it out. "I don't know."

"So what, are you the last survivor of some ancient order or something? Or you're trying to start one of your own?"

With her waking eyes, Liz saw the man sprawled across the alleyway, rivulets of his blood diluted by the rain drops trickling in between the cobblestones. It was so vivid, she almost felt the rain.

"She didn't kill me," the man said, gasping for breath as Liz tried to help him. "She was in such a haste..." He broke into a fit of coughing. "She had somewhere she needed to be. She left me here..." He broke off and clutched Liz's shoulder with a strength that startled her. "Elizabeth. There is no time."

"Mom? Are you all right?" Portia watched her mother with alarm. She'd never seen her mother like this—lost in some world of her own—and it scared her. She reached out and held her mother's arm. "Mom?"

Liz pulled away in obvious distress. "I have to get home," she murmured. "She'll find them."

Now Portia was really frightened. She grabbed her mother's arm again with a firmer grip. "Mom! Snap out of it!"

Liz looked at her in surprise but, seeing the recognition in her eyes, it seemed to Portia she was back in the here and now.

"Are you okay, Mom?"

Liz let out a breath. "I'm okay, honey. I just—" Again, the right words failed to reveal themselves. "I'm sorry. I don't think I can do this right now. I need to think about some things first."

Portia nodded and slid herself back onto her pillow. "It's all right. I think I'm too tired anyway."

Jay awoke with a start and took a moment to realize he was on his sofa. On the TV, he saw the end credits of some show he had no recollection of. The ceiling light seemed way too bright. And there was some irritating noise coming from somewhere nearby...

Rubbing his eyes, he found the source of the annoyance on the coffee table. It was his cell phone.

"Yes?" he said, answering it.

"Hi, Jay. It's Liz."

Jay frowned. Portia's mom? His lecturer in literature?

Hazy images gathered in his thoughts, recollections from an hour or so ago. Liz was in one of them—shooting a girl dead with a crossbow...

No. Not a girl. A creature straight out of fiction.

"Jay?"

"Liz?" Jay winced as he heard himself ask this. Of course it was Liz. She'd just said she was Liz.

"I'm just calling to see if you're all right. Portia was worried about you. So was I."

Jay closed his eyes. He felt too exhausted right then to be shocked, upset or confused. "I'm all right. What about Portia?"

"She's with me. She's asleep."

Her voice sounded odd, Jay thought. He guessed she was pretty shaken up right now as well.

"Are *you* all right?" he asked.

There was a moment's hesitation on the other end of the line.

"Don't worry about me, Jay. Just take care of yourself."

"All right," Jay said, unconvinced.

"Good night."

"Good night, Liz."

Jay put the phone down. No, she wasn't all right. None of them were.

"Kyle!"

Blinking from the bright fluorescent lights in the station, Kyle looked around and saw Alex.

He was passing him a coffee. "Here. You look like you need a pick-me-up."

Kyle took the cup. "Thanks, Alex."

Alex frowned. "Are you all right? You look beat. It wasn't that serious, was it?"

Kyle looked at his partner. It was *very* serious. But he couldn't tell him that. After several years of investigating and a number of transfers, he'd found what he'd been looking for. He'd seen a vampire with his own eyes. Seen her turn to dust. But Alex would never believe that. And if he did, what then? What was the law in relation to vampires? Was it a crime to kill them? Could you put them on trial? Were they counted in the census? Or were they even technically alive?

He didn't know. And until he did, he couldn't say a word to Alex about what had happened. Even if it meant leaving the case officially unsolved. Not that he worried about recognition. He wasn't looking to build a reputation. But to pretend he'd failed when he hadn't... It hurt a little more than he thought it would.

"No, it wasn't serious," he said with a shake of his head. "It's just been a long day and I couldn't sleep last night for some reason."

Alex sighed. "Well, this should cheer you up. There's been another victim." He passed Kyle a photo.

Kyle furrowed his brow as he saw the young woman sprawled across... not a sidewalk or a parking lot. It looked like the small dock area just a little north of the town.

"This is impossible," he muttered.

Alex shrugged. "Why?"

Because Liz just killed the vampire, that's why.

The thought went unuttered. And as he looked at the picture properly, Kyle realized it wasn't impossible at all. The careless manner in which the victim had been abandoned and the jagged wound on her neck were incongruent with the manner in which Ivana had left that kid on the sidewalk. Which could only mean one thing. There was another vampire.

Liz would be thrilled.

The rain was heavier now. Spilling over the roofs of the houses and running down the gutters like streams. Liz ran beside them, lifting her skirt by the hems so as not to trip on it.

There was a lot of noise from somewhere nearby and the glow of torches bathed the buildings all about her.

But the street was empty.

She wondered where the noise was coming from then stopped.

The door to her home was in pieces. Just the bottom corner remained hanging onto the frame in desperation, while the rest of the pieces were strewn across the floor.

Liz swallowed and felt a sudden chill,

Her home, so familiar to her, filled her with foreboding. She had been there and might still be inside.

Then another terrible realization crept over her. She *could not have entered the house while its occupants still lived unless they invited her in. And as her parents would never have done such a thing, then it was too late to warn them. They were dead.*

Liz's lips quivered and tears welled in her eyes. She took a deep breath and let it out. Right then she wanted only to collapse where she was and let her grief pour out but she couldn't. Not yet.

There'd be time to mourn for her mother and father soon but she was not safe here. However, she still had to decide whether or not to enter the house.

On the one hand, even though the door had been broken down, the old book her parents had left for her might still be there. But on the other hand was the terrifying prospect that she *might be inside. Perhaps reading it herself or tearing out the pages. Or perhaps waiting for her to come looking for it.*

Before she could make up her mind though, Liz's legs carried her of their own accord and she stepped over the threshold into what was no longer her home.

With the flickering light of the torches nearby, it was not nearly as dark inside as she'd expected. And while she saw a wooden table overturned and several drawers on the floor, there was nobody in the room aside from herself.

Without making any unnecessary noise, she looked into the other rooms of the house and saw they were empty as well. Then she made her way to a small cupboard beside the kitchen. The doors were open and it was empty.

She let out a sigh. So that was that then. The book her parents had left for her was gone. She *had taken it or burnt it, and now there was no need to stay.*

But, Liz wondered as she stepped out into the brightly lit street... Her half-formed thought abandoned her. Where was all that light and noise coming from?

She looked down a nearby alley and saw torchlight and silhouettes in the square. That's why the streets were so empty. The whole town was in the square, gathered together in a mob.

Liz knew enough of mobs to know she should have turned away and left that instant. But her curiosity drove her on and, with cautious steps, she approached the square.

The noise of the crowd was deafening now. The light of hundreds of burning torches crept up the walls and buildings surrounding the square. The crowd was upset. They were angry and afraid. They were looking at something dangling in the air...

Liz tilted her head up to see what it was as well and was struck by a wave of nausea and dizziness.

Her mother and father, their bodies limp and lifeless, were hanging upside down above the angry mob below..

Liz woke with a start and, sitting up, wiped her eyes and her cheeks. They were wet with tears.

The bedroom door flung open and Portia came in, finding new reserves of strength even in her exhausted state and putting her arms around her. "Mom! Mom! What's wrong?"

Portia felt overwhelmed as her mother leaned into her embrace. Just a few hours ago, she'd told her how she'd been a lot of people over many years. Now it seemed that she could be a lot of people over the course of one night.

And this show of grief was much worse than her sudden lapse earlier.

Unable to think of anything else, Portia took her mother by the shoulders and shook her gently. "Mom!"

It took a moment or two but bleary-eyed, Liz looked up at last, seeming a little more like her old self.

"Portia?" She closed her eyes and let out a heavy sigh. "I woke you up, didn't I?"

"It's okay, Mom," Portia told her. "Really."

Liz shook her head. "No, no. You need sleep. I'm sorry you had to see me like this."

Portia frowned. "It's all right, Mom. You had a bad dream. It's not your fault."

Her eyes still closed, Liz sighed again. "It wasn't a dream."

"What was it then?"

Liz opened her eyes again. "Not now. Maybe in the morning. Go back to sleep, honey."

Portia got up, looking rather unhappy. "But will you be okay?"

Liz contemplated the question. It seemed everyone was wondering that tonight. Jay. Now Portia.

"I don't know," she admitted. "I've got a few things I need to think about and these sudden flashbacks aren't helping." She paused for a moment, frowning. "Or maybe they are."

Portia looked perplexed. "What do you mean?"

Liz shrugged, feeling a bit more composed now. "It's just a thought. But maybe they mean something."

Sleep. It was the one thing everyone needed. And the one thing no one was getting.

Kyle rubbed his eyes as he got out of the car, grateful that Alex was driving.

He'd been right back at headquarters. The crime had taken place at the docks. He could already smell the salty air. It'd be pleasant if he were here under any other circumstances.

He sighed as he took in the whirling blue lights, the yellow police tape and the small gathering of forensic specialists gathered in a circle. These were *not* nice circumstances.

Alex stood beside him. "What do you hope to find here, Kyle?"

"I don't know," Kyle confessed. "Nothing good at any rate. Although, it's funny you ask since coming here was your idea."

Alex shrugged. "True. But what would you listen to me for?"

This got a little smile out of Kyle but it didn't last. It couldn't with the scene before them. Although the sight did confirm his initial conclusion after seeing the photo of the victim. Ivana hadn't killed this girl.

"You know," Alex said, taking a deep breath. "With cases like this piling up, I could almost believe the rumors myself. Who does this kind of thing to someone?"

"*What* does this," Kyle murmured.

"Huh?"

"I think the question is *what* does this."

Alex shook his head. "It's just a prank, Kyle. It's sick and twisted. But it's a prank."

Kyle turned to him. "Three victims, six months ago. Puncture wounds on their necks. Their bodies drained of blood and with no evidence of what happened to it. A couple of nights ago, another victim. Same circumstances. This victim is the fifth. In under a year."

"So we've got a pattern killer or a copycat," Alex said. "It's unusual, sure, but—"

If Kyle hadn't felt so tired right then, he might have let it go. But his resolve to stay quiet was crumbling.

"And the one in Los Angeles last year was a coincidence?" he interrupted. "And the two in Amsterdam at the start of the year? The several cold cases in Slovakia that have only recently been reopened? You said it the other night, Alex. And you know what? You're right. These *are* my kinds of cases. And they're not like other homicides."

He stopped and took a moment to compose himself.

"Well, I don't know, Kyle," Alex replied. "Maybe there is something there that isn't in the textbooks but without hard evidence..."

Kyle sighed. Alex, he knew, was quite right.

Without hard evidence, what he'd seen that evening amounted to no evidence at all.

He couldn't talk to Alex about Ivana. And while he could use the department's resources to track down this new killer, he had no idea just what he and his colleagues could do if they found the creature.

He needed Liz.

But first, he realized, he needed to sleep.

Thursday

IT WAS LATE MORNING WHEN LIZ SAT DOWN TO breakfast. She'd called in sick a few hours earlier, although she knew that only solved the problem for today. She was going to need some leave. And then there was Portia's enrolment. And Jay's. She wasn't his mother but she couldn't help feeling responsible for him as well.

Extended leave. Unpaid leave. Deferred studies. She put it all out of her mind and took a sip of nice warm coffee. It may have been late in the morning but it still felt too early in the day to deal with all that.

Across the table, Portia nibbled at a slice of toast in silence, one small bite at a time. She took another bite. And another.

"How are you feeling this morning?" Liz asked, deciding some conversation was called for.

Portia paused, mid-nibble. "All right, I guess." Her eyes glazed over a little. "I still miss Ivana. I know she had me in her thrall or whatever you call it. She had some kind of power over me..." She frowned. "It's why I couldn't talk to you properly on the phone yesterday, isn't it? When you asked me if Ivana was staying with me?"

Liz sighed. "Yes. But I'm sorry I did that to you."

"No, it's all right," Portia told her with a slight wave of her hand. "You had to know. I just meant..." She broke off and her gaze drifted down.

"I know," Liz said. "You miss Ivana. And it's not just the fact she had a hold on your mind. You saw her die. And to see that, or even just to know it's happened... It's not an easy thing to deal with. Human or vampire."

"I guess."

"It's just going to take some time."

Portia laid the remains of the toast on her plate and looked at her mother. "But it's *not* just going to take some time. We can't just put this behind us and move on. Vampires seem to be a big part of your life. And now it looks like they're going to be a part of mine. You've involved me."

Liz stared back at Portia, stunned for a moment by the strength of her accusation. And that was indeed what it was.

She took a deep breath to compose herself. It was all happening too soon. She wasn't ready for this conversation any more than she was for everything that had happened last night. But then again, Portia would want to know one day. Why *not* now?

"You were already involved, honey," Liz said at last. "When I found you."

Portia frowned. "When you adopted me, you mean?"

Liz shook her head. "I'm talking about before that. I didn't find you at an orphanage. I found you in a street in Seville. Twenty years ago." She looked Portia in the eye. "Right after a vampire had killed your parents."

Portia took a moment to find her voice. "And when were you planning to tell me this?"

Never had been the original plan, Liz thought. And it had seemed like a good one. But perhaps it had been flawed all along. She had never been a big believer in destiny but as she looked at her daughter, the most precious thing to her in the entire world, she wondered if there hadn't been some inevitability to all of this.

"I didn't want to tell you," she said, deciding to be frank. It was obvious Portia wasn't in the mood for sugar coated answers. "I thought you'd be happier not knowing."

"I think I was," Portia said, nodding. She took a deep breath. "But I also think I need to know. Mom, what if there's a connection here? Between my birth parents being murdered by a vampire and what happened with Ivana. I mean, why was she grooming me to be her... her companion? Her bride? What was so special about me?"

Liz considered this. "It could have been random. Vampires are capable, in their own way, of love. Or at least being drawn to others. Maybe she just saw you by chance and that's all there was to it."

Portia frowned. "You don't believe that. And there's more to it. What if Ivana targeted me to get to you? Did she know who you are?"

"I'm not sure," Liz admitted. "I wondered the same thing."

For a moment, it seemed there was nothing more to say. Portia picked up what was left of her toast, prepared to finish it off, then stopped.

"Mom. Who's *she*?"

Liz frowned. "What?"

"Last night," Portia said, "when you were having that nightmare or flashback in my room... The one when you were still awake... I remember clearly. You said you had to get home or *she'd* find them."

Liz opened her mouth and closed it.

"Were you talking about Ivana?"

"It wasn't Ivana," Liz said with a shake of her head. "It was someone worse. You see, there's a—"

A knock on the door interrupted her.

"Oh, for fuck's sake," she muttered, climbing to her feet.

"Maybe it's Jay," Portia said, looking rather shocked that her mother even knew that word, let alone used it.

. . .

It wasn't Jay.

Liz squinted at the visitor standing almost silhouetted against the bright morning light. "Kyle? What are you doing here?"

"I need to talk to you about something." Kyle frowned, glancing over her shoulder at Portia sitting at the kitchen table. "Is this a bad time?"

"Yes, it's a bad time," Liz said, stepping back to close the door. "You shouldn't be here."

Kyle put his hand out. "Wait."

Liz looked at him. "Yes?"

Kyle leaned closer and lowered his voice. "There's been another vampire killing."

"It couldn't have been Ivana?" Liz asked.

"No. This happened last night. Can we talk?"

Portia, it seemed, must have caught a little bit of the conversation because she got up right then and left the table.

"Go on, Mom," she said. "I think I need to have some more sleep anyway."

Liz watched her go then turned back to Kyle. "I can give you an hour. But not here."

. . .

They settled on a local coffee shop of all places. But it wasn't too busy and they found a quiet outdoor table with a perfect view of a handful of palm trees and a half empty parking lot between them.

"Well?" Liz asked once the coffees were on the table and the waiter had left. "Tell me about it."

"The victim was a young woman this time," Kyle replied. "And she was found near the docks all sprawled out. There was something..." He shook his head. "I don't know. It's not the right word but it seemed like there was something... *artistic* about the way Ivana left that kid on the sidewalk the other day. Still awful but it seemed like... you know."

Liz nodded. "I get what you're trying to say. Ivana respected her victims."

"Yeah," Kyle agreed. "That's it. And this new killer doesn't." He took a sip of coffee and gave Liz a quizzical look. "Did you *know* Ivana?"

Liz shrugged. "Not well. Mostly by reputation. She was born as a Styrian countess in 1685. Ivana Karnstein. And judging by her appearance, she probably became a vampire around the age of twenty."

Kyle pondered this a moment.

"Now is there anything else you can tell me about this girl you found?" Liz asked before the conversation had a chance to get sidetracked. It seemed to her that Kyle would want to know more about Ivana's history and how vampires aged. And as far as she was concerned, that would have to wait.

"Forensics found fingerprints," Kyle said. "And they didn't match Ivana's. And the time of death was around 7:30 or 8.00. And that's pretty much everything I've got at the moment."

"Well then," Liz said. "I'll look into it."

Kyle frowned. "That's it?"

Liz studied him in silence for a moment. "What do you mean?"

"I thought perhaps you and I could work together on this. I mean after last night... I thought I would have earned your trust. I took care of everything for you. Including a pretty big pile of paperwork. I covered up your involvement. Both you and your daughter's. And I took one for the team in letting Ivana's case go. And while I know it probably doesn't mean that much to you, I've had a pretty good streak these last few years so throwing a case like that kind of hurt. Professionally speaking."

Liz sighed. "So I owe you one, is that it? Look, Kyle. If that's what you're saying, you're right. I do owe you one. And I'm grateful, believe me. But this isn't a matter of trust. You've earned my trust and then some. That's not the issue. But all your rules and procedures... None of these things were written with vampires in mind. These creatures are outside your jurisdiction. You can't arrest them. You can't hold them against their will. At sunset, they gain the equivalent strength of twenty adult men. If you'd tried to put Ivana in handcuffs for instance, she might have snapped you in two. There's only one way to deal with situations like this and I've been doing it for longer than you can imagine. So leave it with me. Go back to your friends and your family. Live your life. And forget about all this."

Kyle gazed at Liz with a look that was both sad and... yearning. "I don't have a family," he said in a much quieter voice than before. "It's part of the reason why I became a police officer in the first place. And I can't forget about this. I don't *want* to forget about it. Liz, I've spent years looking at these kinds of cases. And despite all the other theories being thrown around to explain the telltale signs away, I've always been sure of my convictions. I knew that if I just kept at it and followed the evidence, I would find the truth. That these creatures are real and that they're living among us. And last night, I found it. I saw it with my own eyes."

"Oh, my god," Liz muttered, rolling her own eyes. "You're enamored with the things. You think they're some otherworldly beings and your ticket to a life of mystery and adventure. Maybe some romance as well. Maybe you've already pictured yourself in the arms of someone like Ivana as she offers you the gift of immortality."

Kyle averted his gaze but Liz saw that the words had stung him. "Maybe some of that's true," he said, looking into his lap. "But I'm not romanticizing these creatures." He lifted his head, his eyes meeting Liz's once more. "But they *are* fascinating. They can live for centuries. You said yourself that Ivana's been alive since the late 1600s. And whether or not law enforcement agencies are equipped to deal with them, they still kill people we're entrusted to protect. I can't just sit back and let them get away with that."

Liz folded her arms but said nothing.

"And there's more," Kyle continued. "Because whether you let me in or not, I'm still going to try to get to the bottom of this latest case."

Liz pushed her chair out and got up. "Well, it sounds like I can't stop you, Kyle. But don't say I didn't try to warn you."

"You won't help?" Kyle asked, getting up as well.

"Help you get yourself killed? No. I don't want that on my conscience, thank you very much."

"All right," Kyle said. "But could I ask just one small question before you go?"

Liz glanced at her watch. "Make it quick. I don't want to leave Portia alone too long."

"I understand. I just have a theory I want to run by you. That's all."

"All right."

"Is it possible that the vampire who did this was the kid Ivana killed?"

"No." The answer came without any hesitation.

Kyle frowned. "You sound pretty sure of yourself. How do you know? Have you been to the cemetery to see whether the grave's been disturbed?"

"Fledgling vampires don't wait to be buried," Liz replied. "The transformation is more or less instantaneous. The idea of vampires rising from the grave is just a superstition that can be traced back to people in the past getting shocked by what appeared to be unnatural changes to bodies after death. Blood pooling around the mouth of a corpse lying face down. Skin shriveling around the nails to make them look enlarged. Stuff like that."

"That's disgusting."

"You're not wrong," Liz agreed. "Now is that all?"

"Well, as far as the case goes. But I want to know... What's your role in all this?"

"That's a longer story."

"I'd like to hear it one day. If you're willing to let me in."

So there *was* romance, Liz decided, factoring in Kyle's attraction to all of this. Only he hadn't been imagining himself in the arms of a vampire maiden.

Well, she couldn't fault him for whatever feelings he might have toward her. And he was, after all, a good man, which counted for something. But still...

"Maybe," she said, giving him a little bit of hope to cling to. Even if it was only a fool's hope.

She turned away, feeling a pang of sadness. It'd be nice to have someone like Kyle beside her. She definitely thought from time to time about the idea of being with someone. But it was impossible. For a moment, she pictured the two of them together with Portia. A family. But even as she imagined it, the vision faded.

"Let's go," she said. "I'm worried about Portia."

There was no conversation in the car as Kyle drove her back to her place. Not that it was a long drive, but there was time for a least a token amount of chitchat.

"Well," Kyle announced once they arrived. "Here we are."

Liz looked out the window and saw this indeed was the case. There was her place and there was her...

She frowned. "My car's missing."

"Maybe your spot was taken last night," Kyle suggested while looking around. "Maybe you had to park further up the street."

"No, I know where I parked my car," Liz insisted. "It was right here."

"You think it's been stolen?"

Liz shook her head. "No. But I think I've got an idea what might have happened to it." She turned to him. "Would you mind waiting here a minute? I might need another lift."

"I can wait," Kyle told her.

"Thanks," Liz said, getting out and walking at a brisk pace.

She opened her front door, marched through the kitchen and living room and found Portia's bedroom door open. Portia, to her total lack of surprise, wasn't there.

A few seconds later, Liz was back outside. She climbed into the car again and closed the door.

"Portia's taken it," she said. "And I'm pretty sure I know where. Go down the street and take a right at the next junction."

Kyle pulled away from the curb. "Sure thing."

Portia had tried to sleep. She really had. But as much as her body needed the rest, her mind was still swimming. And it had been caught in a rip.

So she just found herself doing things. Taking her mom's spare keys. Climbing into her mom's car. And heading round to Jay's on autopilot even though she was—strictly speaking—driving, not flying.

After pulling to the side of the street, she ambled across the sidewalk and knocked on Jay's door.

He didn't take long to answer it. And while he looked pretty groggy, he was awake enough.

"Hey," Portia greeted him.

Jay ran a hand through his hair. "Hey. Um... You want to come in?"

"No, I just want to admire your doorframe," Portia replied.

"Oh."

"That was a joke, Jay," she added when she realized he was just standing there.

"*Oh.*" Jay stepped back and waved her in. He closed the door behind her. "You know, I thought you were supposed to be resting. Liz called me... I mean, your mom called me up last night. She was pretty worried about you."

Portia sighed and sat down on her friend's sofa. "I know. Believe me. It's just there's a lot on my mind."

Jay shrugged and sat beside her. "We were almost killed by a vampire. That's a lot to take in."

"No." Portia shook her head. "It's not that. Although that's plenty already. It's my mom. I've never seen her like that. Like last night, I mean."

Jay contemplated this in silence for a few moments. "Yeah. Well, it seems your mom's a woman of many secrets. The way she handled that crossbow..."

"That was the easiest thing to deal with," Portia said. "She's a guardian apparently. A member of some ancient order or something like that. Killing vampires is like a calling for her and teaching literature to undergrads is just something she does to pay the bills. But after she... After she killed Ivana and we were talking at home, she started acting really weird." Portia turned to Jay with a sudden intensity in her gaze. "She was scared. I've never seen her like it. For a moment or too, she didn't even know where she was. Then later, she woke up crying in the middle of the night. She'd had a nightmare or something but it wasn't like her at all. As in I've *never* seen her like that before. She's always been my hip young mom. Cool. Fun. Laid back. All those things. It was hard to believe."

Jay frowned. "So you can't remember her ever having an episode like that? In your whole life?"

Portia shook her head. "Never."

Jay was quiet for a few moments, staring at the floor as if looking for inspiration before turning back to her. "When she woke up crying, did you ask her what that was all about?"

"She'd had a bad dream, like I said." Portia then closed her eyes for a moment. "Actually, no. It wasn't a dream. I think it was more of a flashback. As if everything that happened last night has stirred up a lot of painful memories."

Jay shook his head. "Well, it sounds pretty rough. I guess you and your mom are going to have a lot to work through. But—" He frowned. "Why are telling me all this? I mean... I'm not trying to sound like I don't care. I do care. It's just that... Well, it seems like something that's private. You know. Something that should just be between you two."

Portia sighed. "I know. You're probably right. But I need to talk to someone else just so I know I'm not crazy. And there's no one else. You know what happened last night. You found that kid the other day. You saw what Ivana was capable of. I mean, who else can I talk to? Matt? He'd think I was making the whole thing up."

"No, we can't tell Matt about this," Jay agreed. "But what can *we* do? I mean, you and me? If you want to figure things out with your mom, I think you need to just make the time to talk through everything with her. Just ask her to put it all out on the table."

Portia thought about this. "There could more on the table than I can handle. It feels like there's too much already."

Jay frowned. "What do you mean?"

Portia opened her mouth and stopped. Just the other day, she'd been sitting with Jay in her mom's lecture hall listening to him and Matt talking nonsense. Nothing deeper than a wading pool. And here she was about to tell him all her fears...

Then another memory came to her. Jay coming through the door as she lay in Ivana's arms. Distracting Ivana and almost getting killed for it.

As if triggered by the memory, Portia now felt the tiny wounds in her neck Ivana had left. She rubbed them with a soft brush of her hand then took a breath to calm herself.

"Ivana isn't the first vampire who's come into my life." Aware of Jay watching her but unable to meet his gaze while she struggled with the emotions trying to grab hold of her, Portia stared ahead. "Mom told me this morning that a vampire murdered my birth parents. That's why she took me in. And so I'm wondering if there's a connection. And, if Mom's been secretly dispatching vampires all my life, then why is she suddenly having these flashbacks now? Or if she had them before, why are they upsetting her so much now? And when I think about it, it seems like the only thing that's different is that I was involved this time."

"She's probably worried about you," Jay said.

Portia took another calming breath and let it out. "Yeah. I'm sure that's part of it. But it seems like Ivana is some kind of sign. A trigger. An omen or something like that. I feel like after last night, Mom's afraid of something. Or someone. And it isn't Ivana. This morning, she was going to tell me. There's someone worse. She was in one of Mom's dreams."

She turned to Jay and clasped his hands. "You've got to promise me you'll be careful. We're not safe any more. And the reason Mom didn't tell me the whole story this morning was that she had a visit from that police officer who was there last night. There's been another killing already. Another vampire. Something's not right. So promise me you'll be careful."

"All right," Jay said.

Portia gripped his hands tighter and looked deep into his eyes. "Promise me, Jay."

"I promise," he told her. "I'll be careful."

Portia let go and stood up. "Good. That's all I wanted to talk about. At least for now. We might talk some more later but I'd better get back home before Mom finds out I'm gone."

As she went to the door, there was a knock on the other side.

Portia sighed as she ran through the possibilities and realized there weren't many. Unless Matt had skipped class early, it was either a salesperson, a postal worker or—and this was where Portia was putting her money—her mom.

"Too late for that, I guess," she said aloud. She turned to Jay as he got up as well. "Remember, not a word to Matt about this."

Jay nodded. "Don't worry. I'm not crazy." He opened the door to find Liz standing outside.

"Oh, hi Liz."

Liz gave him a little smile. "Hi, Jay. How are you holding up?"

"All right," Jay said. "Just need some time, I guess."

"Make the time," Liz told him. "And if you want me to talk to the university for you, let me know. You've got my number."

Jay frowned. "Postpone the course?"

"I can't tell you what you should and shouldn't do. But you've had a couple of pretty traumatic experiences. We all have." Liz put a hand on his cheek. "Think about it." She then turned to her daughter. "Portia, I thought I might give you a ride home. Since my car's outside." She added the last bit a little pointedly.

"Sorry," Portia said. "I just needed to talk to someone."

Liz reached over to her and put an arm around her shoulder. "It's okay. You're not in trouble. I just want you to get some more rest." She noticed the tiny wounds on Portia's neck and frowned. "Did you rub your neck there?"

Portia sighed. "No, no... Well, just a little."

"Try to leave it alone."

"Why? Will it get infected or something?"

"No, but it'll heal faster if you don't touch it." Liz guided her daughter through the door, turning to Jay as she left. "Thank you, Jay. And don't forget what I said."

. . .

"So what did the nice young police officer want?" Portia asked when they were in the car.

"Nothing," Liz said. "He just wanted to clear up a few things, that's all."

"It wasn't nothing," Portia told her. "There's been another vampire killing."

Liz glanced at her then turned her focus back to the road, biting her lip. "You weren't supposed to hear that. And if you weren't eavesdropping, you wouldn't have."

"I wasn't trying to. It's just... I don't know."

Liz let out a breath. "Sounds like Ivana left you with slightly heightened senses. It's a common side effect when a vampire tries to turn someone. There's a reason why it made its way into folklore and some of the famous stories."

"I suppose there's a grain of truth in most of them," Portia suggested.

"Many, yeah."

"So..." Portia tried, feeling a little daring. "The new vampire killing?"

"It's got nothing to do with you," Liz told her shortly. "Ivana was different. She had designs on you. This vampire—whoever it is—isn't coming near you."

"And you can guarantee that, can you?"

There was still a hard set to Liz's gaze but Portia saw tears in her eyes as she spoke. "I won't let them come near you."

Witnessing her mother's fierce desire to protect her, Portia felt a little overwhelmed.

"Why don't you let me help you?" she asked. "Train me? Teach me how to do what you do?"

Liz sighed. "It doesn't work like that."

"Someone taught you though. Doesn't it follow that someday you'll teach someone else?"

Liz didn't answer.

"Mom?"

They came to a red light.

"When I was a few years younger than you," Liz said, "a man came to my parents. A guardian. Somehow he gained their trust and, after a while, he gained their friendship too. And he was very kind to me. I remember that. He taught me a little bit about what guardians do and when I was old enough, he was going to teach me everything I needed to know. He left an old book with my parents for when the time was right."

The light changed and Liz pulled away again. "But he was killed before I was ready to begin. He died in my arms. And when I rushed home to warn my parents, the book was gone."

Portia looked at her with a pang of sympathy. "And your parents?"

Liz saw them again and it was though she were right back in the square. The people who had nurtured and raised her. The two people she'd loved more than anyone in the world. Their bodies strung up for all to see.

And the crowd turning on her. Blaming her. Chanting for her death. At the darkest moment of her life. At the time when she most needed comfort and companionship, she was forced to flee for her life. To run and run until, exhausted from physical exertion and grief, she curled herself up on a lonely moor and shivered in the cold as the rain fell down.

"She killed them too," Liz said, her voice soft. "And she framed me for their deaths."

She. Again Portia wondered at that single pronoun. This morning, her mother had seemed ready to explain who it was that was troubling her dreams and even her waking thoughts. But now it seemed the time wasn't right.

"I'm sorry," she said. She wanted to say more but she couldn't think what more there was to say.

Then another thought struck her. If her mother hadn't begun her training, and if the book that guardian had left her had been taken or destroyed...

"Wait," she said. "You were never trained yourself."

"No."

"Then how do you know—?"

Liz sighed. "I don't. I don't know if I'm doing any of this properly. I don't know if I'm supposed to train someone else to take my place one day or how I'm supposed to find a successor. I don't know about *any* of it."

"What if it's..." Portia opened and closed her hands as if trying to grab the right words out of the air. "I don't know. What if it's something like destiny? You just find the person. And what if it's already happened?"

Shaking her head in bemusement, Liz smiled and glanced at her daughter. "What if it's you, you mean?"

"I'm serious," Portia insisted. "Maybe it's the reason you found me. Maybe this was supposed to happen. You've never thought about that?"

Her mother's smile faded. "I've thought about it. I've thought about it a lot. And maybe I could teach you a little bit. But I just *can't*... bring myself to leave you with a life like mine. You have no idea what it's like."

They turned a corner and were now in their street.

"Well, tell me then."

Liz pulled over and stopped the car. "Guardians don't die of old age, Portia. Not unless they're killed or they pass their gifts on to someone else. I became a guardian on a rainy night in 1693. And I've been one ever since." She took the keys out of the ignition and opened the door, signaling an end to the discussion. "And that's not anywhere near as great as it sounds."

. . .

Home again, Portia's fatigue caught up with her, overcoming her curiosity. She'd been right in what she'd said at Jay's place. There'd been too much on the table already for her to handle. Her mom, a member of some ancient order that fought against vampires. The death of her birth parents. Her *mom's* birth parents. The similarities too striking to ignore. What her mom had been through. The nightmares or memories that were upsetting her. And now, the knowledge that her mom was ageless just as Ivana had been. And in the middle of it all, the enigma of that single ominous word. *She.*

This morning, Portia had been desperate to know the identity of this mysterious woman—no doubt a vampire—who was troubling her mother. Now she wasn't so certain. Ignorance was bliss, as the expression went, and she sure missed it right then. In fact, she wanted nothing more right then than to wind the clock back to the start of the week.

But the reality was that her world had changed. Things could not go back to the way they were and she was going to have to accept it. So for now, she would rest. And tomorrow, hopefully, she'd be able to look at it all with a clear head.

Taking a look at the clock on the wall, Portia saw it was just a bit after midday. If she could sleep all night and wake up at eight in the morning, that'd be a good twenty hours. And if she didn't have any dreams, then so much the better.

One stray thought came to her though as she opened her bedroom door. While she was worried sick about her mother, or perhaps because of it, she wasn't grieving for Ivana any more.

When Kyle came into the office, Alex was waiting with a knowing smile. "Good afternoon, Lieutenant. How was your morning?"

"Why?" Kyle asked, indulging him a little. "What have you heard?"

"Oh, I just happened to pass a familiar looking car this morning. And I thought I saw you with a nice young lady." He fluttered his eyebrows. "Were you getting a little bit of off-duty police work in?"

"No. Just a bit of socializing."

"A date?

Kyle shook his head with a smile. "I don't think I'm quite there yet, Alex." He nodded to some bits of paper scattered across his partner's desk. "Any leads?"

Alex raised his eyebrows. "On which case? The new murder or that one from the other day we haven't solved yet? You do realize we don't just drop cases once a new one comes along, right?"

"No, but I'd like to take this one too. Besides, the two might be related."

"Different perpetrators though," Alex reminded him. "With different styles."

"Which could mean a lot or nothing at all," Kyle replied. "I still say we should take it."

Alex shrugged. "You're the boss. Oh, wait... That's the chief, isn't it? We'd better ask him." He gave his partner a searching look. "But before we go and knock on his door, I want to ask *you* something."

"Shoot."

"What is it you're really after? Why do you insist on moving all over the place to check out these cases?"

Kyle looked him in the eye with nothing but sincerity in his gaze. "Because I'm a believer, Alex. I think there are creatures out there that walk among us... That look like us and talk like us. Dangerous creatures that we're not equipped to deal with. They hide in plain sight because no one believes they exist, mocking us and our morals. Decency. Kindness. Compassion for others. They think they're above all these things. Above the rest of us. And God knows what they think of our petty little laws."

Alex pursed his lips. "You mean Wall Street bankers?"

Though he wasn't in the mood for jokes, Kyle smiled at the quip despite himself. "Well, they may be the same species as the things I'm thinking of."

"I'm sure they'd drain your blood if they could. They drain everything else they can get their hands on."

"True."

"But I get what you're saying," Alex said. "Vampires. Living it up. Getting away with murder because everyone thinks they only exist in books and movies."

"Yeah, that's what I'm saying."

"And you want to bring them into the light, so to speak?"

"Basically. Although I might have left out that pun."

Alex looked at him for a moment and laughed. "You kooky conspiracy theorist."

Kyle's mouth dropped open. "Wha—?"

But Alex clapped a friendly hand on his shoulder before he could say anything. "Just messing with you, Kyle. I don't think you're crazy. At least, I don't think you're any crazier than the rest of us. Come on. Let's go and talk to the chief."

Making as little sound as possible, Liz opened Portia's door and looked inside the room. Her daughter appeared to be in a deep sleep but she wanted to be sure before she headed out for her afternoon errand. She watched her for a few long moments then turned to leave.

The thought cut into her like a knife from behind. She'd left her parents at home when she'd gone to meet the guardian who was supposed to have been her guide and mentor. And it had been the last time she'd seen them alive.

Liz summoned all her strength to banish the thought to the furthest realms of the earth. This wasn't the same thing. Home was the safest place for her daughter right now. And, besides, *she* was thousands of miles away.

But as she reached this link in her chain of thought, Liz wondered. Ivana targeting her daughter. The sudden resurgence of her most painful memories...

And the fact there had been five people murdered by vampires in this little town in under a year.

Vampires, while real enough, were far from common. They didn't multiply like rabbits. Quite the opposite. They rarely felt the urge to swell their ranks and Liz had found certain individuals even killed other vampires in their perceived territories.

What was going on in this town was peculiar and more than a little disturbing. And the more she thought about it, the more it seemed to Liz that *she* might somehow be involved.

But Liz knew she'd just have to cross that bridge when she came to it. Besides, she'd already had a busy afternoon arranging leave for herself and deferring Portia's studies and there was still another job to do.

She closed her daughter's door, wrote a short note and left it on the kitchen table. Soon, she was driving for the dock and the area surrounding it. There were some bars and nightclubs close by and vampires, in her experience, had a thing for those kinds of places.

It wasn't a long drive but she had a brief stopover to make on the way. She got out of the car and got back in a minute later with a bouquet of flowers.

When Liz arrived at the dock, she saw a few crates and a loading jetty in the distance. It wasn't much of a dock in her opinion. She'd seen the docks of Liverpool in their heyday and this one wasn't so much a pale imitation as it was an imitation of an imitation... of a model someone saw in a museum once. However, this at least meant she didn't have to look around too far.

It also explained why—when Liz lay the flowers down at what seemed like an appropriate place—Kyle just happened to be right there.

"That's a nice gesture," he said, coming over from a raised block of concrete he'd been sitting on. He nodded to his right. "If you put them about eight or nine feet that way, I think that'd be just about it."

Liz did so, though she wasn't happy to see him right then.

"Were you waiting for me?" she asked, making no attempt to hide her irritation. "If you want to investigate this murder, that's fine. But don't follow me everywhere."

"That wasn't my intent," Kyle told her. "I was just doing what I usually do at the start of a case. I like to have a look at the crime scene once forensics and all my colleagues have cleared out. I try to think how the victim ended up there and let my imagination fill in the blanks. Why there? Where were they before? Where could the killer have wandered in from? What's nearby?"

"I like to do that too," Liz said. She started walking back to her car. Kyle walked beside her but she didn't say anything to dissuade him.

"Although," he replied, "I imagine when it comes to vampires, you've got a few more tricks up your sleeves than I have."

"Some," Liz said in a nonchalant tone as she reached her car. "Well, goodbye again. And thanks for the ride this morning."

Kyle gave her a polite smile. "You're welcome. Where are you off to, by the way?"

"I'm running my own investigation," Liz told him before she turned the ignition. "Remember?"

She *did* have a few tricks up her sleeves. Kyle was right about that. One was that as a guardian, she always knew if someone was human or a vampire. And whether she'd been born with this sense or if it had been passed on to her by that guardian all those years ago, it was never wrong.

She also knew—or rather, knew *of*—quite a few individual vampires and so she had a list of usual suspects in cases like this. She knew their reputations and habits. Occasionally, she could recognize them by sight. And she remembered a fair few names as well.

As she got out of the car at her first stop and spied a poster on the side of the nightclub there, she saw one name she knew very well.

Eddie and the Living Dead.

Liz glared at the poster. She knew Eddie. Emboldened by a slew of vampire books over the years, numerous movies, TV shows, Halloween parties and pop culture memes, Eddie had taken to playing his vampiric nature up for entertainment—mainly his own—and turning things that people couldn't account for into his parlor tricks. He'd even monetized the fact that vampires didn't show up in photographs by charging fans to try to take a picture with him. And his fans loved it and left his shows amazed. For all the wrong reasons. God, Liz hated him.

But there was one good thing about him showing up at Palm Beach like this. It meant she could dust him.

She stepped back from the poster and looked at the sign on the roof. *The Shack.* The letters were formed from fluorescent light tubes in surfing-esque font and looked like they'd glow red after sunset. Wondering if she'd stick around to see that, she looked at the poster again.

Saturday Night. 11pm.

Liz frowned. Were these clowns playing this Saturday or was that an old poster? With a sigh, she went to find out.

She found the entrance around the corner of the building and went in. No one carded her because there was no one at the door. In fact, apart from one bartender, the place was empty.

It looked to Liz like many other nightclubs she'd seen. The walls and ceiling were painted black. The floor was concrete in some places and covered in patches of miscellaneous material in others. And at the other end, there was an empty stage with obligatory curtains and lights that appeared to be left running all day. Liz wondered if the bill for that was passed onto the patrons in the prices of the drinks or if the young guy wiping down the counter at the bar just liked the look of them. The club also seemed pretty spacious but empty places often did. After dark, it was probably another story.

But since all these musings weren't getting her anywhere, she made her way over to the bartender.

"Hey," she said.

He looked up and gave her a smile. "Hi. What can I get you?"

Liz shook her head. "Too early in the day for me. No, I was wondering about one of those posters you've got outside. Eddie and the Living Dead?"

"Oh. You like them, huh?" The bartender sounded surprised.

I've never heard them play and I want the front man properly *dead.*

"Oh," Liz said instead, putting on a bashful grin. "I'm a bit of fan." She guessed the bartender didn't think of her as a punk rock type. Or whatever type Eddie's fans were. He was right of course, but Liz couldn't tell him that.

The bartender nodded. "Cool. So what did you want to know?"

"I was just wondering when they're playing. Is it this Saturday coming up? It wasn't last week or something?"

"No, this Saturday."

"Thanks." Well, that would make things a little easier. Liz turned to leave then stopped. "By the way, have they played any other shows here already?"

The bartender shook his head. "Not here."

"What about some of the other clubs in the neighborhood?"

"No way." The young man was almost bragging. "We would have heard something if they did. These guys draw a pretty big crowd. You won't be the only fan here on the night."

Liz smiled. "Well, that's good to know. It should be a fun night then."

"It should be pretty cool, yeah," the bartender agreed. "And you should stick around afterward and try to get your picture taken with Eddie. I've got a buddy who's tried it twice." He chuckled. "I don't know what Eddie's trick is but it's insane."

He's a vampire, you twit.

"Yeah," Liz said. "I don't know how he does it either. Anyway, thanks for that."

"No problem. By the way, I love your accent. British?"

Liz hid her impatience. If the bartender was flirting with her, it was time to go.

"Yeah. Good guess," she said, turning away.

On the way back to the car, Liz noticed a few more of Eddie's posters. She pulled one off the wall and had a better look at it. The band was all there, though hand-drawn rather than photographed. There was Eddie sporting an ear-ring, a white shirt with a leather jacket and just enough blonde hair to flick around on stage. There were two other guys behind him and a girl. A brunette with long wavy hair, leaning on a motorcycle with an appropriately sultry pout. And they were all pictured against a dark blue background with silhouettes of bats and headstones and a full moon.

It wasn't too tacky, Liz had to admit. Nor was it gory or spooky in any way. It conveyed a bit of punk attitude and playfulness and nothing more. Which was no doubt just what Eddie had in mind. And he'd probably drawn the poster himself. Andreas had said Edward was quite artistic...

Andreas. As Liz got in the car and drove away, she wondered why that name had come to mind just now. Maybe it was nothing more than his connection to Eddie but with everything else that had been going on, she wasn't so sure that was the case.

A chime sounded and Jay got off his sofa. He opened the microwave, pulled out a greasy paper bag and yanked it open. He wondered for a moment about the nutritional merits in having microwave popcorn for lunch — or was it dinner? — and decided he didn't care.

With his meal in hand, whatever meal of the day it was, he slumped back on the sofa and hit the play button on his DVD remote.

He frowned at the TV screen and took a moment to realize the movie had been playing already without him. It took him another moment to remember he was watching cable TV. Although what it was he was watching, even though he'd just been watching it for the better part of an hour, eluded his efforts to remember.

Then he found himself wondering about Portia and whether she was all right. And Liz...

There was another chime. But it wasn't the microwave.

Jay turned the TV down a little and listened. He heard it again.

"Oh, right," he muttered, getting up. "The door."

He opened it to find neither Portia nor Liz.

"Matt," he said, recognizing his friend. "Hey." His gaze drifted to the attractive young woman beside him. A rather alluring brunette in a white singlet top with something written on the front of it. Jay stopped himself from reading it.

"Hey, Jay," Matt said with a little smile. "You didn't show up to class today. Or yesterday."

Jay rubbed his head. "Uh... yeah. I've felt a little bit weird to tell you the truth."

"And I haven't seen Portia on campus either."

Jay frowned a little. Was it just his imagination or was Matt coming across as a bit forceful? It felt like an interrogation.

"Hey, what's with you, Matt?" he said. "She's probably sick."

Perhaps realizing he was putting his friend off, Matt gave a sheepish grin. "Sorry. I guess I was coming on a little strong there. But, you've got to admit, it's a bit lonely going to class without you guys."

"Yeah, well..." Jay wondered what he should say. As he'd spent most of the day in a near catatonic state, he realized that Liz's suggestion about taking some time off was probably good advice. But this wouldn't be a good time to tell Matt.

Laughing, Matt gave him a playful slap on the shoulder. "Hey, don't sweat it, Jay. You look like you've just been to a funeral." He turned to the young lady. "Hey, I don't think I've introduced you to Cassandra yet. We've just started going out."

The brunette smiled. "Hey."

"Yeah..." Jay said. "Hey."

"Cassandra, this is Jay," Matt told her.

Cassandra smiled. "Nice to meet you, Jay."

"Yeah, it's nice to meet you too." Feeling more was called for, he had a look around the back of his brain to see what conversation ideas he could dig up. "Um... So where did you two meet?"

"Oh, we met on campus," Cassandra told him.

"Yeah," Matt said. "I just saw her there playing guitar the other day... You know, Cassandra's in a band. So anyway, I just went on over and..." He and Cassandra exchanged smiles. "Well. It turns out we've got a lot in common. Actually, it's kind of funny in a way... because if you guys hadn't left me all alone on campus, Cassandra and I would never have met."

"Well..." Jay tried not to faint in his doorway. It was tiring being away from the sofa this long. "I'm happy to help, Matt."

Matt chuckled. "Yeah. Hey, by the way, would you like to come out for a drink with us?"

Jay let out a long breath. "Oh, man. I'm really tired. Maybe some other time."

"Oh." Matt sounded a little despondent.

"But I suppose you could come in and have a coffee."

Friday

"MORNING, SUNSHINE."

Portia blinked as she stepped out of her room. 'Sunshine' was apt. She felt temporarily blinded by it.

Liz hugged her and gave her a quick kiss on the forehead. "Hey," she said, smiling at her. "How are you feeling this morning? A bit better?"

"Yeah," Portia admitted. It was true actually.

"See?" Liz asked. "Sleep. Good."

"It's okay, Mom," Portia replied. "You don't need to use single word phrases."

"No, but they're fun." Liz pinched her cheek. "Muffins?"

"Yes, please. But for the love of God, stop doing that."

"All right, sweetie."

Portia gave in and let her smile break free. Even if her mom was just trying to make her feel better, it was nice to have her joking around like old times...

Except it wasn't like old times. There was no going back to the way things were.

Portia's smile faded as she sat at the kitchen table. But not wanting to bring the mood down, she tried to think about it in another way. Her mom had been a three hundred year old vampire hunter as long as she'd known her. That hadn't changed. The only difference was she hadn't known about it before and now she did.

She sighed as she realized this didn't make her feel any better. Then she realized something else. She would one day grow older, physically, than her mom. And when she died...

"Stop it," she muttered, batting away a stray tear.

Liz turned around from the stove, frowning. "What's wrong?"

"Nothing."

"Well, it doesn't look like nothing. Come on. Tell me. What's wrong?"

"I was just thinking," Portia said with some effort, "when I grow older, you're going to stay the same age as you are now. And when I die, you're going to just live on for centuries or however long, fighting vampires, and I'm going to be a distant memory." Her voice wavered as she spoke and more tears came to her eyes as she finished.

Liz came over. Crouching down, she put her hands on Portia's shoulders and looked her in the eye. "I don't know what's going to happen in the future, honey. But I do know this. You're my daughter and you'll always be my daughter. And you will *never* be a distant memory."

"But what was your plan with me?"

Liz was visibly taken aback by the question. "What do you mean?"

Portia for her part felt overcome by a sense of exasperation. "What do I mean? What do you think I mean? I think you made it clear yesterday that you had no intention of training me up to be your successor so why *did* you take me in? Why did you drag me into your fucked up life? Especially when you knew full well you were going to outlive me. Couldn't you have just dropped me off at an orphanage and left me in Seville?"

Liz didn't answer and, in the ensuing silence, Portia felt her emotions cooling.

"I'm sorry," she said when she felt they were in check. "I shouldn't have gone off at you like that."

But there was no anger in Liz's gaze. Just concern for her daughter. "It's all right. I know this is a lot to deal with. And, to be honest, you're dealing with it better than I thought you would. But if you want to know the truth, I never had a plan. It just felt like the right thing to do." She smiled again. "And it hasn't been all bad, has it?"

"No," Portia conceded. "But it's just... I don't know. I feel like I've been orphaned again." She hung her head for a moment then looked up at her mother. "But if you trained me and passed on everything to me—however you do it—that might make everything all right. Because if you want to know what's really killing me about all this, it's that I don't seem to have a place in this. I mean, you live forever and hunt down vampires. And I'm just supposed to put this week behind me and try to live a normal life."

Liz stood up. Again, she made no reply.

"I mean, think about it," Portia insisted. "Yesterday, you told me you never learned what you were supposed to do next. But the guardian who passed his immortality onto you clearly had a plan to make you his successor. Maybe that's somewhere in that book you told me about. Maybe that's what guardians are supposed to do. If whoever that big shot vampire is hadn't killed your mentor, would he have lived forever after passing his gift to you? Because I'm betting that's not the way it works. Am I right?"

Liz was silent a few moments longer. "Yeah," she said at last. "You're right. He told me many times that when he gave me his immortality, he'd be mortal again."

"So?" Portia asked. "See what I mean? Maybe this is what you're supposed to do."

Liz sighed. "I've thought about it already, Portia. Many times. Since the day I found you. But you said it yourself, remember? My 'fucked up life', as you so succinctly put it. Well, you're right. It is fucked up. It's long. Lonely. I meet people I care about. I grow attached to them. And then I watch them get older and die, while I have to just keep going and keep my chin up. I have to move around, getting used to new places and changing customs. I have to make new backgrounds for myself. New names. Elizabeth Anne Shaw. Kathleen Elizabeth Bradshaw. Elizabeth Marie Benet. Maria Elizabeth Benet. Elizabeth Leigh Garner today. Someone else tomorrow."

Put like that, Portia had to admit, it didn't *sound* like a lot a fun.

"What's your real name?" she asked, her voice soft.

"Elizabeth Soames."

"That's pretty," Portia told her.

"Thanks, honey. But do you see where I'm coming from? I don't want to give you a life like that. And what kind of mother would I be if I did?"

For a moment, Portia was drawn back to their conversation on Sunday night about her new place. *You can't shelter me from the world forever, Mom.* Her words seemed quite apt now.

"Okay," she said. "You don't want to give me a life like that. I get it. But you can't protect me from everything that's out there. No mother can."

Liz contemplated this. "Well, all right. But there's a hell of a difference between letting you stand on your two feet and burdening you with immortality."

"Then don't," Portia said. "At least, not yet anyway. But let me in. Tell me about your life. Tell me about vampires. Teach me how to fire your crossbow. If we're not a normal family, then why should we pretend to be one?"

Liz looked at her daughter in silence for a moment. "All right. I suppose there's no harm in it."

Portia smiled. "Good. Then tell me about your case."

"The one the nice police lieutenant was discussing with me yesterday?" Liz asked, raising her eyebrows.

"Yeah, that's the one," Portia said. "The one I wasn't supposed to know about."

"Okay."

Kyle sat at his desk with a poster for *Eddie and the Living Dead* beside him and a music review site on his computer screen.

"Howdy, partner."

To his internal shame, Kyle almost jumped. He turned around with a smile. "Morning, Alex."

"Working hard?" Alex asked him, nodding to the monitor. "Or hardly working?"

"This?" Kyle asked, looking back at it too. "It's connected to our case. The evidence is still pretty shaky though." He turned back to Alex. "Where have you been this morning?"

"Investigating our other case," his partner replied, pulling up a chair. "The one from Monday night you keep forgetting about. We should at least give it a week before we close it, shouldn't we?"

"Of course," Kyle agreed, smiling. "But since I don't have any further leads on that one right now, I'm following the leads I *do* have."

Alex grinned and took a sip of coffee from a plastic cup. "I'm only messing with you, Kyle. However, before you tell me all about how the 'Living Dead' were behind each and every murder, there's been another one."

Kyle sat upright, every bit of his shock evident in his expression. "What?"

"Last night. A guy named Danny Strass. Well... Daniel. But we know him as Danny."

"You know him? He's one of ours?"

Alex shook his head. "He's been in and out of the station a few times. Got a rap sheet a mile long. A dealer. A rapist. Probably a few other things. To tell you the truth, I can't say I'm sorry he's gone."

Kyle moved to get up. "Should we go and check it out?"

Alex put a hand on his arm. "No. It's already been cleaned up. A garbage man found him in a dumpster. But he matches the others. Puncture wounds on the neck. Drained of blood, with no evidence of where it went. You know the deal."

Kyle nodded. "Except this time the body was disposed of out of sight. And the victim is a felon."

"So let me guess," Alex said. "You think it's yet *another* perpetrator?"

"I don't know for sure," Kyle replied. "But that's where I'm putting my bet."

Alex shook his head and smiled to himself. "So three cases then. And I thought this was supposed to be a quiet precinct." He turned his attention to Kyle's computer screen. "Now, you want to tell me what you've got there?"

Kyle turned back to it as well. "I'd be happy to. What I've *got* here is a suspect. And possibly evidence of something else. This is a European punk rock band. Eddie and the Living Dead. Two of the members—our main man Eddie and the one girl in the group, Cassandra—somehow entered the states without immigration knowing about it. Possibly because they don't appear in photographs and therefore don't have passports."

Alex laughed. "Like vampires, you mean?"

Kyle nodded. "Like vampires. You can check out the website for yourself. I've also visited a few of their fan forums. Eddie's got a party trick apparently. People try to take their photographs with him and he's never in the picture. And Cassandra, who's just recently joined the band, is in on the act as well."

"It could be a coincidence," Alex suggested, though he sounded a little less sure of himself now.

"I'm very skeptical about coincidences, Alex."

Alex swallowed. "I don't know, Kyle. This might sound like I'm making fun of you but I'm beginning to feel the same way. And I'd say more than a few of the others are too." He spread his hands when Kyle looked back in surprise. "I'm not saying I'm a true believer or anything but..."

"With all the evidence stacking up, it's hard to see it any other way?" Kyle asked.

Alex sighed. "Well, I remember what you said the other night when we saw that girl. She was the fifth victim this year. This guy in the dumpster's the sixth. And I've been looking at some stories of similar unsolved cases around the world online." He gave Kyle a little smile. "Your kinds of cases. Some of the ones you told me about, like in Slovakia. A few others as well. And it just got me thinking. If there *are* vampires out there, we couldn't be helping them more if we tried. It seems we'll bend over backwards making elaborate theories to explain their crimes. Bodies have been hung off jetties to let the blood drain drop by drop and Forensics have managed to get the time of death wrong by several hours. Blood has been drawn out bit by bit with a syringe. And most of these theories are more far-fetched than vampires could ever be. The only thing is..." He trailed off, wincing as he tried to find the words and couldn't. He tapped his forehead. "I can believe it up here." Then he tapped his chest. "But I can't feel it *here*."

As he listened, Kyle felt emboldened. Alex, and maybe some of the other officers, were ready to believe what he already knew. They just needed to see the truth with their own eyes. And now he could show them.

He reached out and held Alex's arm. "Let's go and talk to Chief Hardgrave. We'll get a few of the others and go and track this 'Eddie' down."

Alex frowned. "Why?"

"I want to see his party trick firsthand."

"The photo thing?"

Kyle nodded. "The photo thing."

"All right," Alex said. "Although I wonder what the chief will make of it."

Kyle did too. However, while Chief Hardgrave heard him out with a fair amount of skepticism, he wasn't outright dismissive.

"Well," the chief said when he was finished, "I can see where you're going with this, Kyle. However, I also know that this vampire business is a bit of a thing with you. This is the reason why you got your transfer here to Palm Beach in the first place, right? You heard the rumors. Read the reports."

Kyle nodded. "That's right, sir."

"So one could say your interest in this isn't purely objective."

"They could. And they'd be right." Kyle leaned forward and put his hands on the chief's desk. "But these cases of people turning up without a drop of blood left in them... They're real and they're not some one-off occurrence. Every cop in this precinct knows about them and they're all a little unsettled by them. If anything, this plan might do everyone some good. A chance to just find out one way or the other if the rumors are true. And finally, if I'm wrong about this hunch of mine, we lose nothing. We'll have blown off some steam and I'll just go back to the drawing board and try something else."

Chief Hardgrave considered all this in silence for a moment and shrugged. "What the hell. Kyle—I mean, Lieutenant Destri. Let's do it. You can pick your own backup—just as long as everyone in the team's on the same shift—and I'll get your warrants ready."

"Thank you, sir."

The chief nodded and picked up the phone. "All right," he told Kyle and Alex with a wry smile. "Go on. Get out of here."

"So Eddie has a gang with him?" Portia asked. "Possibly?"

Liz shrugged. "Well, he's got a band at any rate. I don't know about his old gang. I've killed some of them already but there are others that might still be out there."

"So what's your plan? Go along tomorrow night, wait for the show to finish and shoot him with your crossbow?"

Liz gave her daughter a wayward glance. "You sound way too interested in this."

"Well, it's new for me," Portia pointed out.

"I suppose that's fair," Liz conceded. "But yes, that's pretty much the plan. Although I might be able to kill him before the end of the show."

Portia shuddered a little. "Do you have to say 'kill'?"

Liz gazed at her. "That's what I do to vampires, Portia. And I don't think sugarcoating it is a particularly healthy thing to do."

Portia wasn't quite sure what to say to that. But since there was a knock on the door right then, she was saved the trouble.

"I'll get it," Liz told her, walking over to it. She expected it to be Kyle. She was wrong.

"Oh," she said, smiling. "Jay. Come on in."

Jay smiled back, though looking a little awkward about it. While Liz was his friend's mom and was pretty cool, she was also one of his lecturers. When he stepped inside and saw Portia, he looked visibly more relaxed. "Hey Portia."

"Hey, Jay." Portia frowned. "You look terrible."

Liz also looked concerned. "I'm going to have to side with Portia on that one. Have you been getting anywhere near enough sleep? Are you eating enough?"

Jay blinked and rubbed his forehead. "No. No to both questions. I feel like I've been sitting on the couch all week surviving on microwave popcorn."

"Well, why don't you stay the day?" Liz suggested. "Have lunch and dinner with us. Have some proper fresh meals. It'll do you good."

Jay thought it over for a moment. "Uh... Yeah, sure. Thanks, Liz."

Liz smiled. "Great. Now, to what do we owe the pleasure of your company?"

"Actually," Jay said. "I wanted to see you."

"Well, come and sit down," Liz told him, guiding him to a kitchen chair. Portia sat down as well. "So what's going on?"

"I think I need to defer my studies," Jay replied. "I feel like a mess."

"I'm not surprised," Liz said. "You've been through a lot this week. Portia's deferring her studies too. And I'm taking the semester off as well. Another professor's coming in next week to take over the classes."

Jay looked at them both. "Oh. Okay. That's good." He turned his attention back to Liz. "Anyway, I remember when you were at my place, you said—"

Liz put a hand on his. "I'd be happy to handle it, Jay. Just leave it with me."

Jay looked at her. "You sure?"

Liz nodded. "I'm sure. There'll be some things for you to sign and they'll probably want to talk to you on the phone but I can handle most of the talking and getting the right forms for you."

Jay looked at her with an expression of genuine relief and gratitude. "Thanks, Liz."

"My pleasure." Liz climbed up. "Now, would you like a cup of coffee or something? Or tea, if you want something more soothing."

Jay thought about it. "You know, a tea sounds good."

"Great. Would you like any milk or sugar?"

"Yeah." Jay's gaze drifted to a small poster lying on the table. "Milk. One sugar."

As Liz put the pot on, Jay picked the poster up.

"What is it?" Portia asked him.

Jay showed her. It was the poster for *Eddie and the Living Dead* that Liz had brought home. "This girl," Jay said with a smile, pointing to the one girl in the group. "I think this is Matt's new girlfriend."

Overhearing this, Liz stopped what she was doing and came to have a look as well. She picked up the poster, frowning. "What was that, Jay?"

Jay looked at her in puzzlement. "I just said that girl... The one in the picture. She looks like Matt's new girlfriend."

"What new girlfriend?"

"Matt came by my place yesterday to see how I was," Jay explained. "He brought along this girl he met this week. She looks just like the one in the picture. And Matt said she's in a band. I think it's the same girl."

Just like Kyle, Liz was skeptical about coincidences too.

"When did he meet her?" she asked, putting down the poster and looking at Jay again. "Did he say anything?"

"Oh, this week."

But question time wasn't over yet.

"Jay," Liz said, leaning closer. "Listen carefully." She glanced at her daughter. "You too, Portia."

Portia leaned into the huddle around the kitchen table as well, both her and Jay's eyes on her mother.

"Did Ivana see you two and Matt together that day when she came to class?"

Portia let out a breath. "Oh, shit. Yeah, she did."

Poor Jay however was still trying to keep up. "What? What's going on?"

Portia pointed to the picture of Eddie in the poster. "This man's a vampire. My mom knows that for sure. And that girl's in his band. She may even be a vampire herself. And given the timing here, it's possible Ivana was liaising with them."

Jay turned a little pale.

"Jay," Liz asked, "did you by any chance invite Matt and his girlfriend in?"

There was no reply.

"Jay?"

This time, there was an audible sigh. "Don't tell me," he muttered. "That stuff about vampires not being able to enter your home unless you invite them in. It's true, is it?"

Portia glanced at her mom then gave Jay a sympathetic look. "Yeah. Mom told me about it. And I can still remember Ivana waiting outside..." She broke off and a tear rolled down her cheek.

Liz reached over and put her hand on her shoulder. "Honey. Are you all right?"

Portia brushed the tear away. "I still miss her. I know I shouldn't but I do." She sighed. "I thought I was over this."

Liz put an arm around her. "You were under the direct influence of Ivana's mind. It takes a while to get over something like that. But you've been remarkable."

Portia nodded. She appreciated the sentiment but it was small comfort when her grief for Ivana felt so real.

Jay got up. "I should go. Give you guys some time alone." He reached over the table and patted Portia on the shoulder as well.

But as he turned away, Liz grabbed his arm. "Wait, Jay. You're not going anywhere."

"But—" Jay looked rather confused. "I think Portia probably needs some time and you two have—"

"You invited someone who might be a vampire into your home," Liz told him. "In fact, you might have invited two."

"Wait a minute," Jay replied. "You're not suggesting that Matt—"

"It's not likely. But without any way of knowing, we'd better be prepared for the worst."

Portia stared at her mom. "Oh, God," she muttered. "This whole thing is horrible."

"It's getting there," Liz agreed, her expression grim. Again, she wondered if *she* was behind it all. After all, *she* was behind so many things. Not content with an immortality bought at the price of numerous lives, she liked to meddle as well. Out of boredom, malice or both. And the games she'd played over the centuries had far reaching consequences. Playing denominations of the church against each other. Inciting Holy Wars and witch hunts. Spurring the worst excesses of colonization. Inciting violent revolutions as well as class and ideological warfare. Even delving into the world of corporate crime, a newer game for the twenty-first century.

Although if sending a bunch of vampires to Palm Beach was another one of those games, Liz had to wonder what the goal was. All the other games she played were like dominos; she'd tap one and watch in amusement as thousands more fell in succession. But this one was different.

"What do you mean?" Jay asked, breaking her out of her silent reverie.

"I mean it's going to get worse," Liz told him. "Anyway, you're staying here. That's settled. But I'll drive you over to your place and you can get your things before it gets dark."

Jay sighed. "I guess that's when vampires get dangerous, right?"

"Right."

"Well, okay then." Jay, wisely or perhaps because he was just too tired, decided not to argue.

"Wait, Mom," Portia called out as Liz picked up the car keys.

Liz looked at her daughter and saw a pleading gaze in her eyes. "What is it, honey?"

"Can you get a few more sets of clothes from my place?"

"Sure," Liz replied. The pleading gaze, she noticed, was still there. "Anything else?"

Portia nodded. "I want my guitar. I know it'll probably sound stupid to you. But I played one of my songs for Ivana and..."

Liz nodded. "I'll get it, honey."

Kyle pulled up in the parking lot and he and Alex climbed out of the car. Behind them, several more of their colleagues did the same.

Alex smiled as he saw the sign on the roof. "Ah, the Shack. Brings back memories."

"Hey, Alex!" one of the others said, grinning and pointing. "There's where you beat the shit out of that guy that pulled the gun on you."

Alex nodded. "Good times."

Kyle rolled his eyes at the banter behind his back. "Oh, brother," he muttered to himself. He turned around and looked at the others. "Okay, you lot wait out here. Alex and I should be able to handle this part on our own. Dave, ask Chief Hardgrave how our warrants are going."

"Right."

Kyle turned to his partner. "Let's go, Alex."

"Right," Alex said, parroting Dave.

"And let's not beat up anyone just yet if we can avoid it," Kyle added.

"Pity," Alex replied as they walked. "You look pretty tough yourself. I reckon we could make quite a team."

Kyle smiled. "I think we already do, Alex."

Inside, they found the place not quite as empty as Liz had found it but not exactly jumping either.

They walked over to the bartender, who looked panicked at the sight of Alex.

He glanced to his left and his right, maybe checking his escape routes, then back at Alex with a nervous smile. "Oh. Officer Rodriguez."

Alex leaned on the counter. "Relax, Trent. You're not in trouble."

The kid breathed a visible sigh of relief. "Well, what can I get you?"

"No, we're not thirsty either," Alex told him. "We're looking for the singer who's booked in here tomorrow. Eddie Blackwell."

"Oh, he's not here," Trent told him.

"What about where we might find him?" Alex suggested, trying to be patient with the kid.

"Uh... I'll get the manager."

• • •

"Cheer up, Kyle," Alex said once they were outside. "We've got numbers. And the boys in the office are working on it from their end as well, remember?"

"You're right, Alex."

"Assuming they're staying in a local hotel or motel, there shouldn't be that many places to call."

"True."

They had now almost reached the rest of their group.

"Are the warrants ready, Dave?" Kyle asked.

"Ready and waiting," Dave replied. "I sent Reeds to pick them up. Where are we taking them?"

"Again," Kyle reminded him, "Alex and I are the ones taking them. Your job is to come in running if anything goes wrong."

Dave shook his head. "I still can't believe we're actually looking for a vampire. What would people think if they found out the Palm Beach cops were chasing ghosts and goblins?"

"And what would they think if we found them?" Kyle countered.

Before Dave replied, there was a burst of noise on the car radio. "HQ to Officer Janowski, come in."

Dave picked up the handheld radio attached to it. "This is Officer Janowski, HQ. Go ahead."

"We've got an update for Lieutenant Destri on his addresses," the woman on the other end told him. "Two band members appear to be off the grid. The other two checked into a motel a couple of days ago and should still be there now. Got a pen?"

Dave hooked the radio over his shirt pocket and got out his pen and notebook. "Go ahead, HQ."

Twenty-five minutes later, everyone had relocated to a street on the northern outskirts of the city, one not so green and leafy as the streets further south. It was wide and sunbaked, with a few units and motels lining its side. Not the kind of place, Kyle thought, one typically associated with vampires.

The other officers fanned out, finding cover behind the occasional bush or sitting in their cars by the sidewalk. And when all was ready, Kyle and Alex made their way up the steps to the second storey balcony of a motel and past three doorways.

At the fourth one, Alex knocked.

A guy with long hair and a goatee answered it. Both Alex and Kyle recognized him as a member of the band. The poster artist had done a very good job depicting his likeness.

"What do you want?" the guy asked.

His accent put Kyle in mind of English footballers he'd seen on the TV. Well, the coarser ones at any rate.

"Hi, I'm Officer Rodriguez," Alex replied, holding up his badge. He nodded to Kyle. "And this is Lieutenant Destri. We're looking for Eddie Blackwell. Is he in?"

The guy in the doorway scowled. "No. Piss off."

"We've got a warrant to search these premises," Alex told him, showing him the document. "As well as a few other ones. So are you going to let us in nicely or do you want to come for a ride with us down to the station?"

"Fine," the man replied, shrugging. "Suit yourself."

"Thank you," Alex told him. He and Kyle stepped past him and found four more people in the living room. Three of them were the other band members. The fourth looked like a college kid and seemed out of place, despite how comfortable he appeared sidling up to the girl beside him on the sofa.

However, their attention was drawn to the guy sitting on the other side of the girl. A guy who looked like a regular punk rock type. His poise and manner gave the impression of a guy with a lot of attitude but there was nothing intimidating or otherworldly about him.

All the same though, both officers felt a little uneasy when they saw him.

"Edward Blackwell?" Kyle asked, taking over from Alex. It was his initiative after all. Besides, it seemed to him that Alex was tongue-tied being in the presence of someone he believed could be a real-life vampire. "You and your fellow band member Cassandra here are under arrest for entering the United States illegally. We need you to come with us."

Eddie stood up, looking nonchalant. "Sure thing, mate. I think we can sort this little misunderstanding out."

Cassandra rose with some hesitation.

The college aged kid beside her, Kyle noted, looked worried, while the other two band members just glared at him and Alex as if they were the biggest idiots they'd ever seen. He chose to ignore them.

The light turned green and Liz pulled away down the avenue. Beside her, Jay was looking out the window and enjoying the view as palm trees lining the sidewalk whooshed by.

"Have you got in touch with your parents at all this week?" Liz asked.

"No," Jay replied, giving her a puzzled look. "Why?"

"Why? You found a murder victim the other day. Then you were assaulted by the woman who killed him. I don't know what a typical week for you is like but I'm guessing this isn't one of them."

Jay didn't reply straightaway.

"Also, if you can't go back to your place until all this blows over," Liz added, "it'd probably be best to stay with them for a while."

"Which one?" Jay sighed. "Should I stay with my dad and mistress number five in the South Hamptons or my alcoholic mother in Florida?"

For a few moments, the only sound was the faint engine of the car and the air conditioning.

"I'm sorry, Jay," Liz told him. "That sounds rough."

Jay sighed. "It's all right. How could you know?"

"So what do you want to do then?"

"Well, if I can't go back to my place, can't I just stay with you and Portia for a while?"

Liz thought about it.

"Look," Jay said, "if you're worried about involving me in all this vampire business, then I think that ship's already sailed, hasn't it?"

"Maybe," Liz said. "But as I said, this vampire business is probably going to get worse."

"Well, I'm not going to my parents," Jay insisted. "Either of them."

Liz gave him a sideward glance. He looked pretty tense.

"All right," she told him. "But I'm only agreeing to this to keep you safe. I don't want you getting involved in the vampire business any more than you've been already."

Jay gave her a smile. "Thanks, Liz."

Liz smiled back. "You're welcome, Jay."

At that moment, Jay's phone started ringing so he pulled it out to see who was calling.

"It's Matt," he told Liz, tensing up.

"Answer it," she replied, keeping her eyes on the road.

"Hey Matt," Jay said. "What's up?"

"These cops just rocked up and arrested Cassandra!" Matt told him without any preamble.

"Huh? What?"

"I said these cops just rocked up and arrested Cassandra!"

"Yeah." Jay scratched his head. "I got that bit but I'm kind of missing some context here. Were you guys at home? And what did they arrest her for anyway?"

"We were at a motel," Matt replied. "Her band members are all staying there. We were just hanging out when two cops rocked up at the door."

"And why did they arrest your girlfriend?"

Beside Jay, Liz's expression was taut.

"They said she entered the country illegally."

Jay pursed his lips, trying to think of what he should say next. "What to do you want me to do about it?"

"Ask him if the cops arrested anyone else," Liz muttered.

"I wasn't saying you should do anything," Matt said. "I just said—"

"Hold on," Jay told him and covered the phone. He looked at Liz. "What?"

"Ask him if the cops arrested anyone else," Liz repeated.

Jay nodded and lifted the phone up again. "Hey, Matt. Just out of curiosity, did the cops arrest anyone else? Maybe they weren't really after Cassandra."

"Yeah, they arrested Eddie."

"And Eddie is?" Jay asked, deciding in this instance it was better to feign ignorance.

"He's the leader of the band."

Jay nodded, forgetting as so many people do that physical gestures get lost in translation on the phone.

"What are we going to do about it?" Matt asked.

"You've got to go," Liz muttered to Jay. "You're at college. Admin stuff. Make something up and do me proud."

"Um... I'm really sorry, Matt," Jay told him. "I've got to go. I'll call you later."

"Jay! Wait—"

Jay hung up.

Liz shrugged as she drove. "Kind of harsh."

"Brain freeze," Jay told her.

They came to another set of lights but they were nearly back at Liz's now.

"So the cops have just arrested two vampires, is that it?" Jay asked.

"That's what it looks like," Liz agreed. She took a deep breath and let it out. "Damn."

At the station, Kyle sat at a small table in the interview room. On the other side of the table, Eddie Blackwell gazed at him in a manner swinging between disinterested and rebellious. He had also rocked his chair back on one leg and was using it as a pivot to spin the chair back and forth.

"Good afternoon, Eddie," Kyle greeted him. He gestured to a glass of water on the table. "If you're thirsty, have some. That's for you. And there's no water shortage in the station."

Eddie smiled at him, picked up the glass and emptied it in one gulp before putting it back down again. His smile broadened. "Thanks."

This in Kyle's mind didn't prove or disprove anything, as he had no idea whether vampires could eat or drink regular things. However, he found Eddie's knowing look intriguing. It seemed to him that Eddie knew full well what he was up to.

Though, whether or not that was the case, Kyle wasn't going to give up his charade so soon.

"Now you said earlier this was all some kind of mistake," he said. "But we have no evidence that you entered the country through any official checkpoints.

Furthermore, several officers searched the motel you were staying at and although we found luggage, we didn't find any passports. For either you or Cassandra. It's pretty unorthodox to travel overseas without a passport, isn't it?"

Eddie remained undaunted. "Must have lost it then."

"Then that must have been a while ago," Kyle continued. "You've played in America before. I've seen tour dates online. Reviews. Discussions about your shows in your fan forums. But again, there are no official records of you entering the country on any of these occasions. Also, your lack of records go back a few more years than Cassandra's." He smiled. "Just joined the band recently, did she?"

Eddie shrugged. "Yeah. We wanted a chick to shake things up a bit. Chicks in bands are hot."

Kyle's smile remained but he made no comment.

"So how 'bout it, mate?" Eddie asked. "You drag me here and ask me all these questions. So what happens now?"

"I'm not entirely sure," Kyle told him. "I don't think anyone's likely to go to jail. Although you might end up getting deported. But if you can reschedule your show before tomorrow... Who knows? Maybe you can get a passport and a visa and be back in a month."

Eddie stared at him with an intelligent gaze. "So what happens now?" he repeated.

"Well, we'll need a couple of things from you and your friend," Kyle told him. "First of all, we need a cheek swab to get a DNA sample. And after that, we just need some pictures. Then you and Cassandra will be staying the night in our holding cell. And hopefully by morning, we'll have this all cleared up."

Eddie leaned across the table, his smile remaining fixed. "You know what Cassandra and I are," he said in a conspiratorial murmur. "And you want us to stay the night with you?"

The words chilled Kyle to the bone and—not for the first time—he wondered if he was in over his head with this. However, years of practice allowed him to keep his fears to himself and not let his expression betray him. Whatever reaction Eddie was hoping to get, Kyle wasn't going to give it to him if he could help it. He fell back on one of his old tricks and gave Eddie a polite smile. "I'm not sure I understand."

Eddie chuckled and leaned back. Again, Kyle wondered just how well the man could read him. It didn't look like he was fooled by any of his pretences.

"My mistake," Eddie said. "So... A cheek swab, eh?"

"And then some photos," Kyle told him.

"Right," Eddie said. "Mustn't forget them."

You'll be exposed, Kyle thought. *You know that, right?*

This unnerved him more than what Eddie had said earlier and he wondered why the man had acquiesced so easily. He remembered Liz's words at the cafe yesterday. *At sunset, they gain the equivalent strength of twenty adult men.*

His colleagues, and in particular Chief Hardgrave, were equally surprised by how readily Eddie had agreed to everything. And the chief was concerned.

"Kyle," he greeted him.

"Sir," Kyle replied. He was standing outside a room with incremental measurements painted up the far wall, looking through the one-way glass at one of the occupants inside. An occupant who looked unconcerned and even amused, as though being there was his idea of fun. He held onto a sign with his name on it, looking as though he'd just accepted an award.

The woman beside him however, also holding a sign with her name, appeared a little nervous—although Kyle doubted she was as nervous as he felt right then.

"I've just been thinking," the chief said. "What if these people really *are* vampires?"

"Well, that's why we're doing all this."

The chief twitched and scratched the back of his head. "Yeah, I know. It's just... When you told me this idea of yours, I thought it'd be a good way to blow off some steam. Like you said. You know, we could all get this vampire stuff out of our systems and then we'd all feel a bit better."

Kyle knew when to talk and when to listen. This was the latter.

"But," the chief said, "I've got this bad feeling. Everyone in the station's wondering now, are these guys vampires? And I'm worried. What if the answer's yes?"

"That's why we're all standing by," Kyle said. "In case there's any trouble."

Chief Hardgrave sighed. "I don't like it."

"Yeah," Kyle agreed. "Me neither." Perhaps, he thought, it was time to change the subject. "Anything from Forensics yet?"

"Yeah." The chief swallowed. "They found a match for Eddie's DNA. Vampire or not, he's a likely match for the culprit who murdered that girl on Wednesday night."

Kyle's expression was resolute. "Then we've got to bring him in, right?"

"I know. But I'm worried."

"I know," Kyle replied. "You said."

Inside the room, Officer Reeds was ready to take the photographs.

Both Kyle and the chief watched him intently. Alex had joined them as well, along with half a dozen more of their colleagues.

"Just face forward," Reeds told their male suspect.

The camera clicked and everyone looked at the little viewing screen on the back of it. Sure enough, there was a photo of the back wall. But there was nothing else.

"Wait a minute," Reeds said. "Let's just try that again."

There was an audible click as the second photo was taken.

"No. Something's not right. Again."

There was another click and another photo with nothing in it but a wall.

"All right," Reeds said, turning the camera toward the woman. "What about you?"

The camera clicked again.

Reeds glanced back at the window behind him, perhaps taking comfort in the fact that there were a dozen officers on the other side watching this. With his face as pale as if his own blood had been drained, he looked like he needed it.

Kyle glanced at his colleagues. They didn't look much better. The chief in particular looked like a man in dire need of a stiff drink.

He swallowed and pointed to the suspects in the other room. "I want those two locked up."

The assembled officers hesitated. They wanted them locked up as well but were all rather hoping that someone else would volunteer to do the honors.

"Now!" the chief snapped.

The assembly mostly scattered and Chief Hardgrave walked away, rubbing his temples.

Kyle stood where he was for a few moments, transfixed by what had just happened despite himself. This was what he'd expected. And Eddie and Cassandra weren't the first vampires he'd personally encountered. And yet...

Again, he felt that dreadful chill and he wondered what on earth he'd been thinking.

He turned around and jogged to catch up to the chief. "Sir, are you all right?"

Chief Hardgrave stared at him. "Am I all right? Your crazy theory was right on the money. There are real vampires and now we've got two of them in the station. How exactly could I be all right?" He turned away. "I've got to go and make some phone calls. This situation's above *both* our pay grades and I don't want the responsibility of dealing with it. And neither do you if you know what's good for you."

Kyle stared after him.

"Congratulations, Kyle," the chief called over his shoulder before slamming his office door shut.

As Kyle stood wondering what to do now and when his brain would regain its full functionality, Alex came over.

"Don't worry, Kyle," he said. "All things considered, I think that all went about as well as expected."

Kyle frowned. "And how well is that?"

"What do you mean? You've proven your little thesis. You've got over a dozen witnesses who saw Eddie's photograph trick and DNA evidence to link him to one of the murders. You've brought these sons of bitches into the light. Hell, you might end up a celebrity because of this."

"Eddie and Cassandra went along with all of this too easily for my liking," Kyle told him.

"They're spending the night in the holding cells," Alex said. "What can they do?"

While it wasn't intended as anything but rhetorical, it was a good question. And while Kyle didn't know the answer, he intended to find out.

"I hope you're right, Alex," he told his partner. "But I want you to keep an eye on them. I'm going to make a call."

He picked up his cell phone from his desk and went out into the parking lot. The sun was going down, he noticed, and it made him even more nervous than he already was. With good cause.

He rang Liz.

"Kyle?" Liz said, clearing some things off the kitchen counter. "What have you done?"

"I've got some news," Kyle said. "I—" He broke off. "What do you mean, what have I done?"

"I heard the whole story, Kyle. Friend of a friend. You've got a vampire in custody. Possibly two."

"It's two. I know."

Liz flung her free hand in frustration. "Great. I mean, what the *hell* were you thinking? I told you I was going to take care of this."

"There were murders, Liz," Kyle countered. "And I'm a police officer. I can't just turn a blind eye to them."

"I understand that but you know the reality of the situation. The police aren't equipped to deal with this type of thing. Where are the vampires now?"

"We've got them in the station holding cells," Kyle told her in his most assuring tone. "They're contained."

"Contained?" Liz exclaimed, unable to believe what she was hearing. "You can't contain them, Kyle. Don't you get it?"

"But if we let them go, they'll disappear," Kyle said. "So we've got to keep them."

And in that moment, Liz realized it was too late.

"Kyle," she told him. "What those two creatures choose to do now is out of your hands. Do you understand me? You've invited them into the station. It doesn't matter if you keep them or release them. By bringing them into the station, you've given them the ability to come and go as they please." As she looked out her window, she saw the last light of the afternoon was fading fast. "Kyle. You've got to get everyone to safety right now. You've got to get everyone *home*."

"What?"

"Get everyone to go home!" Liz shouted. "I'll be there as soon as I can. And Kyle? Hurry."

She hung up and headed for the door, aware that Portia and Jay had been listening the whole time and were watching her.

"Mom, is everything all right?"

"Not even remotely close," Liz muttered, fighting back more tears and an overwhelming sense of anger and frustration.

"Mom!"

"No, you can't come," Liz snapped.

Portia ran over and grabbed her arm. "I didn't mean that," she told her. "I meant, be careful."

Kyle rushed back inside and found Chief Hardgrave wandering in a daze.

"Sir, are you all right?"

The chief shook his head. "I don't understand it. I made three calls. And every time I tried to explain what happened here, I just... I couldn't. I started saying other things that had nothing to do with it. And I couldn't stop myself. It was like I was a passenger in my own body."

He looked up, his gaze a mixture of disbelief and despair. "Kyle, what's going on?"

Kyle put his hand on his shoulder. "I don't know, sir, but we've got to get everyone out of here. We're not safe."

Chief Hardgrave frowned and pulled away. "What do you mean, we're not safe? We're not going anywhere." He jerked his thumb over his shoulder in the direction of the holding cells. "We've got two vampires in there. We've got to keep them under armed guard."

"It won't do any good," Kyle insisted. "They're twenty times stronger than us."

Now the chief looked at him as though he were crazy. "And where the hell did you get that from? A novel? A movie?"

"Sir, sir," Kyle tried again. "You have to trust me. We may not have much—"

A squeal of stressed metal and a clattering crash cut him off.

"Time."

The chill that had been cutting into him all afternoon had now morphed into abject terror. He drew his gun and ran for the holding cells.

"Get everyone out of here!" he shouted over his shoulder.

There were several gunshots, another crash and a scream that made his heart skip a beat. He rounded the corner of a corridor at full speed and saw a scene of carnage.

Both vampires were out. Several steel bars from the holding cells were strewn across the floor, along with the bodies of Reeds and Dave.

But what struck Kyle the most was the incredible speed at which Eddie and Cassandra moved. It was so difficult for his eyes to track their movements that it seemed they were simply vanishing from one place and reappearing several feet away.

He fired several shots of his own that seemed deafening in the enclosed quarters but he couldn't tell if he'd hit anything. Several of the ceiling lights were now out and smoke from gunfire filled the air, making things worse.

There was another scream and as Kyle tried to see who it was, Alex appeared at the other end of the corridor.

"Alex, stay back!" he yelled but to no avail.

His partner charged at Eddie, firing two good shots. But just as he was about to slam into his target, Eddie stepped aside and grabbed him by the neck.

It all happened too fast for Kyle to react. As he watched in horror, Eddie hoisted Alex into the air, grabbed him by the waist and brought him down — snapping his back over his knee. He then leaned over and, with large incisors that appeared as if from thin air, he bit into Alex's limp neck and raised his head once more. Blood trickled down his chin and it was all Kyle could do to stop himself from retching.

He turned and, without feeling so much as a drop of shame, ran as fast as he could.

"Kyle!"

It was the chief, he knew. Tears streamed down his face as he heard the desperation in the man's voice. But there was nothing he could do.

"Kyle! Wait for me. Ky—" Chief Hardgrave's plea ended in a gurgled scream.

Kyle kept going, kicking the front door open. He felt stabbing pains in his chest and a wave of nausea but he had to keep going.

He dropped his gun—it was no use to him now—then pulled out his car keys as he collided into the passenger door at full speed. Wincing and not daring to look back, he unlocked the vehicle, opened the door and dived in.

The car rocked with a heavy thud and the passenger door slammed shut behind him.

As he climbed into the driver's seat, he saw that Eddie had hit the side of the car just after he'd got in. Eddie, who only this afternoon had looked like a typical wiry young guy, now seemed more akin to a raging lion. He circled the car, grabbed it and shook it. The vehicle swung from side to side and every bit of it rattled. Kyle wondered if it was even still on the ground.

Cassandra, he saw in one brief moment of clarity, was standing aside watching. God knew what she was thinking right then but Kyle was glad she wasn't helping Eddie.

Then with a lurch, the car rolled over. Kyle smashed his head into the steering column and vomited a little.

He screamed as the car was hit again. Blood ran down his forehead.

The whole car shook once more. All the windows were shattered now. Yet, a small part of Kyle's mind noticed that Eddie had made no attempt to reach inside and pull him out.

He let out a laugh, albeit a spluttering and somewhat unconvincing one.

"What are you waiting for?" he cried out.

At that moment, the shaking stopped. Someone grabbed Eddie and threw him back.

Kyle strained to see who was out there. Dazed, lying in an upside down car while contending with the warmth of his own blood and the smell of his own vomit, it wasn't easy. But in the parking lot lights, he saw a man he didn't recognize grappling with Eddie.

The man hoisted Eddie off the ground and slammed him into the hood of another car, exhibiting a strength Kyle recognised as superhuman. Eddie for his part though was far from beaten and in a vicious rage, he fought—tearing a strip of metal off the side of the windshield and stabbing it into the newcomer.

"Oh, God," Kyle muttered as more tears welled in his eyes. "This can't be happening."

After all these years, he'd found vampires. He'd proven their existence to others and to himself. And now he realized it might have been the stupidest thing he'd ever done.

The second man collapsed as Eddie drew the metal shaft out of his side—and it seemed as though the mystery newcomer was finished. Eddie brought the makeshift weapon down on his shoulders with a sickening thud and raised it again for another blow. But before he could inflict any more injury, Cassandra appeared in the parking lot and—to Kyle's complete surprise—grabbed her band partner from behind and attempted to pull him away.

With a little effort however, Eddie pushed her back and raised the metal bar once more to finish off the newcomer…

…and it was in that moment that Liz fired her crossbow. As it had for Ivana, her shot rang true once more and Eddie fell to his knees. With his strength fading, the vampire tried to turn around to see who it was who had ended his existence and seeing Liz, his eyes widened in a startled gaze. She was, she knew, the last thing Eddie would ever see. Then, as she looked on, the vampire's body crumbled and the dust dissipated in the early evening air.

Cassandra, for her part, turned and ran. And Liz was all too happy to let her go. The vampire was more than capable of ambushing her if she tried to follow her in the dark. It'd be much easier to deal with her later on her own terms.

She walked across the parking lot and collected the wooden bolt she'd used on Eddie and tucked it through her belt, any thoughts of hunting Cassandra fading away as she assessed the scene before her. There were two people who needed her help now and that took priority.

She ran to the broken wreck that had once been Kyle's car and opened the door on the driver's side.

"Kyle!"

Her heart skipped a beat as she saw him. This man, so strong and yet gentle, shivering on the ceiling of his vehicle and looking at her with terror and tears in his eyes.

"Liz," he stammered. "Oh, Liz. I'm so sorry."

Liz sighed. "Never mind that now. Let's just get you out of here. No broken bones or anything?"

"I don't think so," Kyle told her.

"Well, let's hope you're right." Liz crouched down, hooked her arms around his armpits and, with a heave, hauled him out of the car.

"It was good thinking, getting inside the car," she told him. "It seems your car is like your home. A vampire can't enter it unless you invite it in."

"I can't say I thought it out that much," Kyle admitted, sounding a little out of breath. "And even if they can't enter cars without an invitation, they can sure shake them around."

"Well, you're lucky you got help when you did," Liz told him, looking over her shoulder at the other injured man. The one who'd come to Kyle's rescue. She felt a lump in her throat when she saw him. Someone from her past. She'd always thought she might see him again someday. But seeing him here at Palm Beach was something of a surprise.

However, as much as she wanted to rush over and talk to him, there was something urgent to take care of first.

She pulled out her cell phone and made a quick call, while keeping an eye on Kyle. "Jay? Yeah, it's me." She had another look over her shoulder. "No, I'm not after Portia. I need you to come to the police station."

Jay said something in reply and Liz took a deep breath.

"It's bad," she told him.

When she finished the call, she put her phone away and patted Kyle on the shoulder. "You all right here for a moment?"

Lying on his back, Kyle nodded. "Yeah. Go ahead."

Giving him a smile of encouragement, Liz stood up to go and check on the other man.

The sound of gunfire was ear piercing and as she finished tending the injured soldier in front of her, Elizabeth Marie Benet wondered if the fighting was getting closer. The tent flap was pulled back and two more soldiers, their faces caked with grime and mud, came in bearing a third man on a stretcher.

Elizabeth glanced down at the man already in her care and then at the man on the stretcher. The former was stable for now. The latter was...

"Bring him here," she said, waving to the two men carrying him.

There were tears in the nearest man's eyes. "You have to help him. He stormed two machine gun nests to save the rest of the men. Please."

"I'll do what I can," Elizabeth assured him, changing her gloves and taking a better look at the wounded man.

He was perforated with wounds and drenched with blood from his neck to his waist. A bullet had grazed his forehead as well and he had several more entry wounds down the length of his legs.

The two men who'd brought him in placed their hands on his shoulder before leaving him, and there was a silent plea in their parting gazes.

Elizabeth tried to give them a smile of assurance but she knew—as they no doubt did as well—that there was little chance she could save the man lying on the bed in front of her. That he was even still alive defied everything she'd learned about nursing during the Great War. But the faint rising and falling of his chest told her that he was, despite his horrific injuries.

And once she was alone in the hospital tent, with the other injured soldier sleeping, and she was able to recover from her initial shock at seeing such stark evidence of the senseless cruelty of mechanized warfare, Elizabeth understood how he'd survived.

"You're not human," she told her patient as she cut away his blood soaked uniform.

He coughed and spluttered, unable to speak, but she saw understanding and what looked like recognition in her eyes. Perhaps he knew what she was as well. Perhaps, she considered almost as an afterthought, they had even met before.

However, she doubted he'd pose any danger to her now. With the injuries he'd suffered, it'd be some time before he'd pose a danger to anybody.

"I hunt your kind," she continued, although she wasn't sure why she was telling him this. "But I don't know... You've just saved the lives of a lot of young men and as I look at you now..." She shook her head. "It doesn't matter anyway. This war is a lot bigger than the two of us. You're English too?"

"These days," the patient replied, forcing the words out with a hoarse voice. He smiled. "But I was a Dutchman back... back when..."

Elizabeth smiled as she prepared to administer a general anesthetic. "When you were human. I understand. Anyway, I shouldn't be making you talk right now. Now, I'm going to put you under for a while but don't worry. I'm not going to harm you."

The man nodded and closed his eyes. Once the anesthetic had been administered, Elizabeth went to work removing the bullets and stemming the bleeding. The latter would be a problem; it would be some time before the man could recover the blood he'd lost. A transfusion would solve the problem but under the circumstances... Improvising, she swept as much of the man's spilled blood as she could into a beaker.

Elizabeth cleaned the wounds and worked fast stitching and bandaging. She just finished before three more wounded men were brought in. And for the next few hours, she was too busy to check on her mystery patient.

It was only in the evening, with the sounds of gunfire retreating in the distance, that she was able to have a few minutes alone with him again.

"Thank you," he told her, his voice still weak but without the strained hoarseness from earlier.

"You're welcome," Elizabeth replied. "Do you feel a little stronger now? This evening?"

"A little," the man admitted. "Although, it may be some time before I'm my old self again. Maybe years. Maybe even longer than that." He smiled. "Provided you don't hunt me down like the rest of my kind."

"I've never met anyone like you among your kind," Elizabeth told him.

"Well, we're not all monsters. Although we've met before. You probably don't remember."

Elizabeth tried to recall the man's face but there were a lot of memories to sort through. So many years and so many places.

"Wait a minute," she told him. "I saw you in Bavaria. You were with that group with Edward the Kinslayer." She scowled as the name passed her lips. Even now, after all these years, it still made her recoil in disgust and horror.

"Only for a short time," Andreas told her, though his tone was apologetic. It seemed to Elizabeth that he shared her revulsion as well. "I left shortly after you attacked us on that hilltop."

"But you were a friend of Edward, weren't you?"

"I was," the man said. "For a time. Despite his faults — and God knows there were many — he treated me with kindness and brought me in when I needed a companion. And he had a gift for art, I remember. I admired that about him. But I never became like him. In fact, in the brief time we traveled together, I tried hard to change him."

"How?" Elizabeth asked. "How can you change the nature of your kind?"

"It's not nature," the man told her with some heat. "There's nothing natural about us. I know that. I can feel it. But the blood lust that comes with being a vampire doesn't define us. It doesn't make us who we are. We decide that. Yes, we need blood but we don't need to drink it often and we can choose how we get it. I try not to drink from the living at all if I can avoid it. And I never drink from the innocent." His gaze drifted down. "Sadly, Edward could never be persuaded to see things my way. He tasted the blood of his own kin, which many say is the sweetest. And once he committed that sin, I don't think he ever had a chance of coming back." He looked at his nurse with grief in his eyes. "Did you kill him?"

"Edward escaped," Elizabeth told him. "Along with some others. And you." She gave him an appraising look. "Although I never did get your name. I'm Elizabeth, by the way."

The man smiled. "Pleased to meet you, Elizabeth. I'm Andreas."

"It's good to meet you too, Andreas. Although I have to ask something. It's been weighing on my mind since your comrades brought you inside. Why are you here? Why are you helping us?"

"I may not be human," Andreas told her, "but this war concerns each and every one of us. I want to help."

"Well, I think you have helped," Elizabeth told him. "And saving the lives of several dozen men is something you can be proud of, Andreas. Unfortunately though, you might not be able to do much more for a while. You've lost a lot of blood and I don't know how long vampires take to heal from wounds like yours. And I think your guess earlier is probably right. It could be years."

Andreas smiled. "So what's to be done with me in the meantime then? I can't go back out there but if I go to a hospital, it might raise a lot of questions. What do you think? Would it be better if regular folk know we exist or is it better the way it is?"

Elizabeth shrugged. "I've never decisively chosen one option over the other. But I think I'm inclined towards the latter. Given that vampires and 'regular folk' look the same, I could easily see common knowledge of vampires leading to another wave of witch hunts. And I never want to see horrors like that again." She sighed. "Or horrors like this."

"Then it looks like we're at an impasse."

Elizabeth was inclined to agree but she thought a little longer before replying. Perhaps there was another option.

"No," she said after a few moments. "You can't go to a hospital and you can't go back out there. You're quite right. But in folklore and stories, vampires are said to rise from the grave. Maybe we can take some inspiration from that. Let your comrades believe you're dead. Disappear from the world for a while and rest until you're strong again. It will grieve your *friends and comrades out there but they'll understand. Besides, they probably don't expect you to survive anyway. I could see the two men who brought you in were already preparing themselves for the worst."*

"I'll never see them again," Andreas murmured.

Elizabeth gave him a sympathetic look. "I know. I'm sorry, Andreas."

The vampire closed his eyes and exhaled before opening them again. "And what about you? Do you think I'll ever see you again?"

"Well," Elizabeth said, "neither of us are getting any older." She smiled at her patient.

"Elizabeth," Andreas murmured, his eyes lighting up with joy as he saw her leaning over him. "You look exactly the way I remember you."

Once again, Liz smiled at her patient. "Well, it's as I told you, Andreas. Neither of us are getting any older."

She frowned as she saw a deep scar along one side of Andreas' forehead and ran her hand along it.

"No," Andreas told her. "It never really healed."

"I'm sorry."

"Don't be. Besides, I'm the one who should be sorry."

"Why should *you* be sorry?"

"I came here to help you," Andreas explained. His voice was a little strained as he fought down the pain while he spoke—but he was managing. "But I foolishly took on Eddie and Cassandra by myself and now I'm going to be a burden to you again."

"Look, Andreas," Liz told him. "You weren't a burden in 1915 and you're not one now." She looked at the wound in his abdomen and gave him a smile. "Besides, we both know you've seen worse."

Behind them, Kyle had risen to his feet. He was a bit shaky but he hadn't lost his hearing.

"1915?" he said, gazing at Liz.

Liz turned to him. "I'll fill you in later, Kyle. I've got someone here I'd like you to meet. This is Andreas. He just saved your life from Eddie."

Kyle frowned. "I saw it. But if he could hold his own against Eddie, then there's only one explanation, isn't there?"

Liz nodded. "That's right. He's a vampire."

Kyle stared at Andreas for a moment and then at Liz. "He's on our side?"

"Yes, he is," Liz told him. "And I think you forgot to thank him for saving you."

Kyle winced and shook his head. He knelt down by Andreas and clasped his shoulder. "I'm sorry, Andreas. It's been a rough night and I'm still just trying to catch up. But thank you."

"It's all right," Andreas told him. "I understand." He gazed at Kyle in pity. "I'm sorry about what happened in there. I wish I could have got here sooner."

"How did you know to come here at all?" Kyle asked, frowning again.

"Cassandra's new boyfriend," Andreas explained. "He's pretty easy to follow." He turned his gaze to Liz for a moment. "And he's much too talkative. He's been trying to get to home base as fast as possible and he's been telling Cassandra everything he can to speed things up. I tell you, I seriously thought about breaking his neck a few times."

Kyle opened his mouth in horror. "I thought you—"

"I *thought* about it," Andreas told him. "I didn't do it, Kyle."

"How do you know my name?"

"Lieutenant Kyle Destri? I know it because I've been keeping an eye on you and your investigations. In fact, I've been reconnoitering ever since I got here."

Liz stared at him. "You've been reconnoitering? Why? What are you up to? You said earlier that you came here to help. Help do what?"

"*She's* coming," Andreas told her. "That's what all these other vampires are doing here. She's sent them on ahead but she's coming herself in case they fail."

Liz trembled as she heard the news and her knees gave way under her. Since she was crouching, she didn't fall far and she managed to stop herself with one hand. But she was still shaken.

Kyle, having not seen Liz like this before, looked worried.

"What does she want?" Liz asked.

Andreas shook his head. "Not here. When we're safe."

Liz took a deep breath to compose herself and climbed to her feet. "All right. When we're safe. Someone's on their way to help me move you and Kyle." She glanced at Kyle as she said this. "Although you're looking a lot better, Kyle. You've managed to get back on your feet pretty quickly."

Kyle exhaled. "Yeah, don't believe it. I feel like a wreck."

"Well, stay here with Andreas then until I get back," Liz told him. "I'm going to look inside the station for survivors."

Andreas reached out and held her ankle.

Liz glanced down, annoyed at the delay. "Andreas, let go."

"There aren't any survivors," he told her. "They're all dead."

"I have to see for myself," Liz replied. "Just in case."

"I'll come with you," Kyle told her.

Liz frowned. "Someone needs to stay here with Andreas."

Andreas shook his head. "No, no. I'll be all right, Elizabeth. As you said, I've seen worse."

Liz sighed. "All right. We won't be long. Come on, Kyle."

The inside of the station looked like a slaughter house. Liz glanced at Kyle every few seconds as they walked through the building. A number of lights had been shattered in the confusion and several small fires were burning, turning the building into an eerie netherworld of flickering flights and deep shadows. It was almost medieval.

Tears welled up yet again in Liz's eyes. The bloodied bodies in the firelight brought her right back to that fateful night in the square all those years ago, with the bodies of her parents dangling above the crowd with their torches... right before they turned on her.

She had exerted her influence on that mob, Liz knew. That's why they'd convinced themselves that a lie was the truth. That's why they'd stirred themselves into a frenzy. And what's why they'd tried to murder her and forced her to flee to that cold wet moor.

And now *she* was coming here.

. . .

The woman, exquisitely beautiful with high cheeks, rounded lips and smooth brown skin, looked like a goddess of the ancient world brought to life. She smiled at the other woman behind the desk.

"Passport?" the woman asked her.

"That won't be necessary," the beautiful stranger replied. "All the nations of the world are my domain."

The woman looked at her in breathless awe. "Yes."

"I am Hasheeba, my child. And I am your queen."

"Of course," the woman replied, bowing her head and looking apologetic. "Please. I didn't mean to delay you."

Hasheeba kissed her forehead and the woman gushed with pleasure.

"There's nothing to forgive, my child," the self-proclaimed queen told her before proceeding through the checkpoint.

Kyle and Liz reached the holding cells where the worst of the violence had occurred and, with moistened eyes, Kyle crouched down beside one of his colleagues.

"I'm sorry, Alex," he told him. "I'm so sorry."

Liz watched on but said nothing. No words of hers would be any comfort here.

Her phone rang and she answered it. "Jay? Yeah, okay. We'll be right out."

She put the phone away and walked over to Kyle. "Jay's here. We've got to go."

They left the station and met Jay outside. By that time, Kyle was in such a state of shook that the fact he'd seen Jay twice before hardly registered. Jay helped him into his car. Then he and Liz lifted Andreas and put him in her car.

"So what's the plan?" Jay asked once they were done. "Just head back to your place?"

"Yeah. I'll see you there," Liz told him.

She climbed into her car and started it up.

"Wait," Andreas called from the backseat. "Can we stop by my motel first? I need to get my bag."

Liz sighed. "Look, we can get you a change of clothes later."

"No, it's not that. I've got something for you. It's important."

Liz wondered what he meant by that but decided it could wait until they were safe at home. "All right. Where are you staying?"

Thankfully, the motel was only two blocks away. Andreas also gave Liz some money to settle the bill and let the owner know he was checking out. Once that was done and they had the bag, they rejoined the others at Liz's place. And as she saw her daughter and Jay wondering what was going on, Kyle slumped at the table in a state of shock and Andreas lying injured on the sofa, Liz thought they must have been the sorriest household in Palm Beach.

"Um, who's sleeping where?" Portia asked. "We've only got two bedrooms. Maybe Jay and I can go back to my place."

At the start of the week, Jay's eyes might have lit up at such a suggestion. Now, he just gave a meek nod in agreement.

"Out of the question," Liz said. "Cassandra's still out there and, according to Andreas here, Matt's told her everything he knows about us."

"But she can't come into my place unless she's invited, right?" Portia countered.

"No," Liz replied. "But I don't want to take any chances. Cassandra and Matt might camp outside waiting to catch you when you go to the shops. Or they might try to lure you out by some other means. Who knows? But Matt's never been here before and I'm reasonably sure he doesn't know the address. So for the time-being, this is the only safe harbor we have."

Jay took a tentative step forward. "Has Matt been turned? I mean, we're talking about the guy like he's one of them. But... for Portia and me, he's our friend."

Liz took a breath. "I don't know, Jay." She turned to the resident invalid on the sofa. "Andreas?"

"He wasn't when I last saw him," Andreas said. "But that was yesterday. Now it's anyone's guess." He shuffled a little bit to get more comfortable. "Elizabeth. I think you should know that this 'safe harbor' of ours won't be safe for long. *She's* coming. And I don't think she's far away."

"Have you been talking to her travel agent?" Liz asked him. "How do you know what her movements are?"

"I think Eddie's concert tomorrow was intended to be a trap for you," Andreas explained. "Edward the Kinslayer. The vampire that got away. You despised him and *she* knew it. If he came here and put himself out in the open, you'd find him soon enough. She could pretty safely rely on that."

Liz frowned. Unfortunately, the theory made all too much sense. "So are you saying Eddie was using himself as bait?"

"That's what I think. And if he was, then you can be fairly certain *she* would have been at his show tomorrow night to spring the trap. Now, I don't think it'll take her long to find out what happened at the police station tonight. And once she does, she'll adjust her plans accordingly. She's not stupid."

"No," Liz agreed. "She may be a lot of things but stupid isn't one of them."

Portia looked at Andreas and then at her mother. "So what now?"

Liz managed a smile. "It looks like we don't need to worry too much about the sleeping arrangements at any rate. Whatever we come up with, it'll only be for one night. Tomorrow morning, we're going to get out of Palm Beach, go to ground and lie low."

Kyle sat up at the table, coming back to the land of the living. "It looks like this woman's got you pretty nervous. Are you sure you're not overreacting?"

Liz whirled about. "This *woman* murdered my parents and framed me for the deed. She convinced a town full of people who'd I considered friends since childhood to try to kill me. And God knows what else she's done in the intervening years. I've only got fragments of the picture but she's stirred up gang lynchings, bloody minded revolutions and wars and it's all in a day's work for her. And those vampires who killed your friends this evening, Kyle, are *fledglings* compared to her."

Judging by the expression on Kyle's face, the words had some effect. "So who is she then?"

For a moment, Liz looked taken aback.

"I mean, you and Andreas keep talking about her," Kyle pointed out. "And you've just told us how dangerous she is. But who is she?"

Liz felt keenly aware that all eyes were on her so she turned around to look at everyone at once. She'd intended to tell Portia about this the other day, she remembered, but Kyle's arrival that morning had prevented her. It was therefore a little funny that Kyle should be the one to remind her that she'd never got around to finishing that conversation. She wondered for a moment if that was ironic, then decided she didn't care.

"If vampires had a leader," she told the sorry group, "then she'd be it. And she already considers herself the queen."

"The queen of the vampires?" Jay asked.

"The queen of the world," Liz replied. "Her name's Hasheeba, and she's the oldest known vampire in existence."

As she said the name, Liz's eyes met Portia's and she saw her daughter's features grow taut even though she'd never heard it before. Liz however understood. She'd felt the same way herself way back when she'd first heard it too. Back before she'd lost her family. It was the reason she avoided saying it.

"And since we're bringing everyone up to speed," she added, "I may as well be honest with you all about myself too. We're all in this together now so no more secrets. We'll work together far more effectively if we share what we know rather than keep it to ourselves. So here goes.

"Now, Portia and Andreas already know this but Kyle and Jay, you don't. I'm what they—whoever they are—call a guardian. It's a little hard to explain properly so I'll give you the short version. I hunt vampires and I don't age. At least physically speaking, I stopped ageing when I was in my late thirties. I became a guardian in 1693 when I inherited the so-called gift of immortality from another guardian, who died. He was my mentor. And I've been hunting vampires ever since."

People tended to need a little time to let a statement like that sink in so Liz gave Kyle and Jay a moment or two before she continued. They'd need a lot longer than that, of course, but time was pressing.

"Now, I don't know how good a job I'm doing since... *Hasheeba* stole a book my mentor had left for me. It was supposed to explain what being a guardian was all about and I never got a chance to see it. But I'm doing the best I can."

She stopped to let everything sink in a little more, gauging the reactions around the room while she waited. Kyle and Jay—little surprise there—were staring wide-eyed and slack jawed. Portia of course knew this already, although Liz saw she was a bit surprised she'd told everyone else in the room about it too. Liz could hardly blame her for that however since a couple of days ago, it had been an intimate secret for just the two of them.

Liz then turned her gaze to Andreas. The vampire, still lying on the sofa, was... Liz looked at him a little longer but, try as she might, she couldn't tell what he was thinking. She gave him a questioning glance but he shook his head and mouthed one word. 'Later.'

Liz turned her attention back to the room at large. If she had to wait to find out what that was all about, then she could wait. "Any questions?"

Jay glanced at Kyle. "I don't know about everyone else here but I think we've probably got enough to digest as it is. Anything more right now would be information overload."

Liz smiled. The kid was level headed, she had to give him that.

"Good," she announced. "Then I think everyone should get some sleep. Kyle, you can sleep in my room. Jay, in Portia's. I've got a couple of spare blankets in the linen cupboard you can sleep on. They're not much but they're better than just sleeping on the floor. And you'll also find some sheets and a few spare pillows in there too. Andreas, I'll have another go at bandaging that wound for you, then you can just sleep where you are. That sofa's pretty comfy. And in the morning, we'll get underway."

"Where are we going?" Portia asked.

"East. South," Liz said. "It doesn't matter where. But we can't stay here."

Everyone seemed to agree with this arrangement with the notable exception of Kyle, who shook his head. "Well, *you* can all go to ground. And I'm pretty sure Andreas lives off the grid anyway. But I've got to let someone know what happened tonight."

"Who?" Liz asked. "I'm not trying to be insensitive here but, honestly, who can you talk to? And what would you say? Assuming you even *can* say anything."

Kyle frowned. "What do you mean by that?"

"I mean if you try to tell someone, you might find that you can't anyway. When Portia was worried about Ivana earlier, she called me up and she couldn't say a *thing* about what was going on. And Eddie's at least as powerful as her."

Kyle remembered Chief Hardgrave back at the station telling him how he'd made those phone calls about Eddie and Cassandra and how he'd been like a passenger in his own body, listening to words coming out of his mouth that he had no control over.

He sighed. "But when the morning shift comes in tomorrow..."

"I guess they'll assume you were killed too," Liz said. "And for the moment, I think it's best to just let them. When the time's right, we'll figure out how you can make your miraculous return from the grave."

Kyle nodded but he didn't look very happy.

"I'm sorry," Liz told him. "But I'm also worried about *her* coming after you as well. I don't know how much she knows about us. And I don't know how much Matt knows either or how much he's blabbed to Cassandra." Liz noticed Jay wincing at her mentioning his friend in that manner again. "But there's a good chance she might use you to get to me. That'd be bad news for either of us but I'd imagine it'd be especially bad for you."

There was another reason as well, Liz knew, but there was no sense in worrying Kyle with it then. Especially as he would probably make things worse for himself if he knew.

The mass of blazing torches blurred her vision. The cries and shouts of over a hundred people became a single sound, rising to a deafening roar.

"Murderess!" they cried.

"Hang the witch!" a sole voice in the crowd shrieked. Others took up the cry, while more threats followed.

They were almost upon her and all she could do was run. She hitched the hem of her dress then tore the fabric from the bottom to move more freely. Still, she felt the mob right on her heels. She felt their collective breath and the heat of the torches.

The narrow alley helped her to get a little way ahead of her pursuers but it wasn't enough. She had to get out of their sight. Taking several deep breaths, she urged herself to run faster. She ignored the pangs in her side and the burning sensation in her throat. Better than the burning sensation of a pyre.

To slow down was death. She repeated it to herself as she ran... across the cobblestones, through the narrow alleys... out over the grassy hills, now sodden with rain.

The dark...

She had often feared it but now she longed for it to envelop her and conceal her from the raving, bellowing mass of bodies pouring out of the town in pursuit.

The hills grew steeper but she pressed on, panting and almost crying from the pain of such exertion.

She was losing the mob now but she couldn't become complacent. Not yet.

With a crack that sounded as though the mountains had been torn asunder, the sky lit up in a brilliant flash. It blinded her for a moment and, startled, she stumbled but quickly picked herself back up. The rain that had been steadily falling now came down as though the heavens had opened.

Ignoring everything—the exhaustion, the aches, the damp and the chill—she pushed herself ever onward and found herself upon a wild moor. Here, she caught her breath and took a chance to look back. At last, she was alone.

To be safe, she continued soon after but this time at a slower pace. Nevertheless, she still tripped over tussocks of grass and concealed rocks. She slid into a tarn and, drenched from head to toe, crawled her way out.

For hours, she wandered in this manner. Exhausted. Hungry and thirsty. Bruised and bloody from stumbling over too many rocks. Soaked through and shivering with cold. When she was too tired to walk any more, she crawled her way into a depression in the soft soil under an overhanging rock. Then curling herself up, hugging her knees to keep off the chill, she let her grief take voice and her crying mingled with the howl of the northern winds blasting across the moor.

With a gasp, Liz opened her eyes and found she was in her bed. All the lights were out and then she remembered the others staying with her. Andreas sleeping on the sofa. Jay sleeping on the floor of Portia's room. And...

She leaned over the side of the bed as it all came back. Kyle, she saw, was sleeping on top of a blanket on her floor. Since he hadn't stirred and no one else in the house had either, Liz felt confident that she hadn't woken up crying or anything like that as she had the other night. It was something of a relief, though only a small one.

She knew full well now why these memories were coming back again. *She* was coming.

With a sigh, Liz tried to put her out of her mind and go back to sleep. A light tapping on the roof sounded like the beginnings of rain. A few moments later, the drops had turned into a downpour. This time though, under cover and on a soft mattress, the noise was soothing.

Saturday

THEY TOOK TWO CARS, LIZ'S AND JAY'S.

Jay drove with Kyle to keep him company, while Liz drove with Portia in the passenger seat beside her and Andreas lying on the back seat.

It was still raining when they left and it was pretty dark. Liz had the windscreen wipers going at full speed.

"You don't get motion sickness, do you?" she asked Andreas.

"No."

"Well, it's not as though vampires eat anything," Portia said. "Right?"

"Oh, we eat things," Andreas told her. "Drink things too. And I never say no to a fine wine."

"Then why do you drink blood?" she asked.

"We have to," Andreas explained. "We don't get any sustenance from regular food and drink. But I still enjoy it."

"Do you miss being human?" Portia asked a few moments later.

Andreas thought about it. "It's been so long since I was human, it's a little hard to remember what it was like now. But yes, I do miss it. I can still pass for human, blend in, make friends and all of that but..."

When it was clear Andreas had trailed off, Portia glanced over her shoulder. "But?"

"But I know I'm not one of you. And I spend my life feeling like I'm watching everyone else through a window."

Portia was quiet for a moment. She glanced at her mom, wondering if she felt the same way. Liz however was just watching the road and making sure Jay was still behind her.

"That must be hard," she said.

"Well, I can't change it," Andreas told her. "so there's no sense worrying about it."

They drove on in silence for a while longer. Portia glanced over her shoulder again and saw that Andreas had closed his eyes.

"Don't worry about him," Liz told her. "He's sleeping. That wound in his side is pretty deep."

"He's going to be all right though, isn't he?"

"I hope so."

Portia looked at the sleeping vampire again. "One of the good ones, eh?"

Liz laughed. "Stop looking back all the time. You'll make yourself car sick."

Portia faced the front again. "It's just weird. A week ago, I didn't know vampires existed. Since then, I've had one try to kill me, another one's murdered a dozen police officers and now we've got a tame one lying on the back seat."

Liz flashed her a stern look. "You should get that thought out of your head right now. Andreas isn't tame. You heard him. He needs blood and if he can't get it any other way, he gets it from the living. In fact, he killed someone just two days ago."

Portia whirled around then looked back at her mom. "What?"

Liz shook her head. "It's all right. He said he saw this guy assaulting a woman in a parking lot. It'd been a long time since he'd last had any blood so he decided to feed. And he probably saved that woman's life in the process. So there's that at least."

Unable to help herself, Portia glanced back yet again.

"Stop turning around, honey," Liz told her. "I told you, you'll make yourself sick."

"Sorry." Portia looked forward once again and tried to focus on keeping her eyes looking that way.

"He's not going to hurt *you*, Portia."

"Well, that's good to know. Although how long are we taking care of him?"

"I don't know," Liz said. "We'll just have to wait and see."

"Also, why would he tell you he killed someone?"

Liz smiled at this. "I guess he figured Kyle might ask about it sooner or later so he thought it'd be better to tell me first."

"Sensible enough."

They drove on in silence a little longer. Portia stopped looking over her shoulder and started looking out the window instead. "So where are we heading anyway?"

Liz shrugged. "At the moment, nowhere in particular. We'll just follow this road and see where it takes us."

Portia pursed her lips. "I think we'll end up in the desert following this."

"Well, we are in California," Liz pointed out. "So it's highly possible."

As it turned out, they did end up in the desert, under a sky that looked almost as dry as the stretches of sand beneath it. The dark gray storm clouds over Palm Beach had now long vanished over the horizon.

They followed, as they drove, a road that wound its way through a landscape that would feel right at home in a Western, then took the first road that left it. Liz thought the whole hiding out idea might work a bit better if they changed direction at least once on the trip.

They crossed a few hills, a dusty plain, a bit of dry farmland and about three and half hours after leaving Palm Beach, they came to a small town.

"This'll do," Liz said, seeing a motel a little bit past a gas station with a lot of open space around it. She stopped at the station first to fill up, as did Jay, and then they rolled a hundred yards or so to their destination.

"What a dump," Portia said as she dropped her bags beside the door to her room.

"It'll do," Liz told her, standing just outside.

She passed a set of keys to Andreas and another to Kyle. "All right. Andreas, you're in the next one down. Lucky seven. And, Kyle, you and Jay are in number five."

"Thanks," Kyle said. "By the way, Liz, I can pay my share for a few nights as well. You don't have to pay for everything by yourself."

Liz patted his shoulder. "Don't worry about it, Kyle. I've been around a long time. I have enough in savings to keep afloat a while."

Kyle frowned.

"What?" Liz asked him.

"I don't know," he sighed. "It's just somehow knowing about your... It's kind of hard. I feel like finding out about vampires was a lot easier for me to deal with."

Liz gave him a smile. "I'm still me, Kyle. I'm still Liz."

Kyle hung his head. "I know. But it feels like now you're somehow... out of reach."

Liz squeezed his hand. "Try not to overthink it. We've got enough to deal with already. Let's rest up for now. We've all had a pretty big week."

In another motel, one back at Palm Beach, Hasheeba—self-proclaimed queen of the world—followed Cassandra into the room she'd rented with Eddie and the band.

A young man got up and embraced Cassandra. "Hey, are you all..."

He trailed off as he saw Hasheeba, his expression a mixture of awe and fear.

"Quiet," Hasheeba told him and although her tone was as nonchalant as if she were ordering breakfast from a cafe menu, the word froze Matt where he stood. She eyed him in distaste then looked at Cassandra's two human band members "You and Eddie keep company with these two?" she asked her.

"Rick's a pretty good bass player," Cassandra explained with a note of apology. "And Leo's the best drummer Eddie and I have had in years."

Hasheeba looked at them both a little longer, while Rick and Leo stared back at her with that same mixture of awe and fear that now seemed permanently imprinted on Matt's features.

"You may go, my children," Hasheeba told them. "The show tonight is cancelled. Leave this country, return to your homes and pray you never see me again."

While Rick and Leo gathered their bags and passports, Hasheeba saw Rick's bass guitar on a stand in the corner of the room. She picked it up, played a rather fast and complex lick with no apparent effort, then put it back. If Leo's drum kit wasn't in the back of a van on the street, she might well have played that as well.

"Nice sounding instrument," she murmured to herself.

Soon Rick and Leo had re-emerged and the bass had been packed away. They left at once without so much as a goodbye and Hasheeba turned her gaze to Matt once more, who still remained frozen where he was standing. "So this is the boy?"

"Yes," Cassandra replied.

"And how much does he know? How much is he worth?"

Cassandra hesitated before she replied. "I don't know. But I'm sure that he's worth more to us alive than dead."

Hasheeba studied Matt in silence for a moment longer before turning away. "You pity him," she said with disgust. "Well, that's your affair. Now, we have more important things to discuss. The plan shall require some alterations."

"Yes," Cassandra admitted. "We didn't count on the police getting involved.

Hasheeba smiled at this. "No, of course you wouldn't. Particularly under Edward's influence. He believed he could use the skepticism of the modern world as a cloak. I remember what he told me once. Let people furbish their own explanations and they'll cover your tracks for you. A catchy motto. But I warned him—and you—that modern skepticism only protects us so far. Edward should not have killed so soon before his show. It was too much."

"But we needed to be certain Elizabeth would come looking for him," Cassandra pointed out.

"But Edward didn't need to kill anyone to do that. He just needed to let Elizabeth know he was here. I *gave* you adequate funds to advertise your show. You should have used them."

Cassandra hung her head. "I'm sorry."

Here though, Hasheeba relented. "It's all right, my child. The mistake was of Edward's making and the price has been paid in full. Now, I must speak to whatever is left of the Palm Beach police force and then we shall visit the home of Matt's friend Jay. Then Portia's. And finally, Elizabeth's."

"Matt doesn't know where Elizabeth lives," Cassandra pointed out.

"I know that," Hasheeba replied. "His usefulness has expired yet you keep him like a lost puppy. But no matter. The police will know."

"Do you think we'll find Portia there?"

"I expect," Hasheeba replied, "that all three places will be empty now."

Cassandra frowned. "What do you mean?"

"I mean our adversary and her companions will most likely have left Palm Beach already." Hasheeba smiled once more, though there was a cruel curve to her mouth. "But that's all right. We'll find them soon enough." She turned to her companion. "But first, let us feed."

Cassandra glanced at Matt, fear in her eyes, then looked back at Hasheeba. "Wait. I'm sure we can find someone to satisfy our appetites."

"I'm sure we can," Hasheeba agreed. "But time grows short. Elizabeth and the girl might already be far away."

"But," Cassandra started. She hung her head in meek submission. "I do pity him."

Hasheeba sighed. "Oh, Cassandra. You've been living with mortals too long. And this one is far from worthy of such a blooming flower as you are. But if it bothers you, think of it this way. His blood will merge with what's left of yours. And in that way, he will remain a part of you. What more could a young man want?"

Cassandra said nothing and Hasheeba turned her attention to Matt. She reached out a hand and, with gentle movements, pulled him toward her. "Come, my child. Serve your queen."

Liz opened the door to Andreas' room and stepped inside. Again, he was lying on the sofa.

"I've bought some fresh bandages," she said. "I thought I might take another look at the wound."

"No, thanks," Andreas replied. "I'd like to just leave it for a while."

"All right." Liz held up a small bag. "By the way, I've also got some more ibuprofen if you need it."

Andreas smiled. "Thanks."

"Well, let me know if you need anything else. Just knock on the wall." Liz turned to leave.

"Wait," Andreas called her.

Liz stopped. "Yes?"

Andreas took a breath. "I wanted to tell you something."

"All right." Liz guessed this was what he'd hinted at the night before.

The vampire nodded to a couple of kitchen chairs a few feet away from her. "You might want to sit down."

In silence, Liz carried one over and sat across from the sofa. "What is it?"

Andreas hesitated. "There's something you should know about Portia." He stopped for a moment to consider his statement before amending it. "Actually, there's *a lot* you should know about her. First of all, I don't think you found her by chance. And deep down, I don't think you do either. You were drawn to her."

Liz frowned. "I was just in the right place at the right time."

"But why were you there?" Andreas asked her. "Why were you in Seville at all? Were you living there at the time?"

"No."

"So you just decided to take a holiday and happened to rescue the little girl who's now your daughter?"

Liz thought it over. "Okay. I admit I did feel something strange at the time."

"Can you describe it?"

Liz sighed. "All right. I felt as though I had to go to Seville and it had to be then."

"Right."

"So what does that mean exactly?"

Andreas nodded to a bag on the floor, the bag he'd asked Liz to retrieve from his motel room. "There's an old book in that bag, Elizabeth. And there's a page in it about choosing a successor. It describes what you just told me."

Liz started to tremble. "Are you saying you've got a book about—"

"I'm saying everything," Andreas told her. "I'll tell you about the book in a moment. But first I'll tell you how I found it. Just before you came to Seville, I was with Eddie and Cassandra's group again."

Liz sighed, her disappointment clearly marked in her expression. "Oh, Andreas..."

Andreas nodded. "I know. But I was lonely. I needed company. Anyway, while I was with them, I learned that *she* had had a vision. Her death at the hands of a young woman. Portia."

Liz drew in a deep breath and let it out. "You mean to tell me," she asked Andreas, "that this *bitch* had a vision of my daughter?"

"That's what Eddie and Cassandra heard," Andreas explained. "And that's what they told me. They believed Portia would become another guardian, like you. So I left them and went to Seville to find out for myself. I was there, Elizabeth, when Portia's parents were killed. And I can prove it because—"

"You killed the killer," Liz told him.

Andreas was taken aback for a moment.

"That's right, isn't it?"

"Um, yes." Andreas got his bearings again and continued. "And as you know, Portia wasn't with them. Now, I had no idea where she was so I went to her family's home to see if she was there. And *that's* where I found that book. Someone had left it for Portia. Which means that even if the prophecy isn't true, the idea that she's supposed to become a guardian might well be."

Liz was quiet for a little while. After all, there was quite a lot to take in.

"So there was another guardian then?"

Though still lying down, Andreas managed a shrug. "Well, that's what it looks like."

Liz nodded. "You think they're still alive?"

"It's probably unlikely."

As difficult to accept as that was, Liz guessed that was the case as well. "So you kept the book then," she said, getting back to the main topic.

"Only for safe keeping." Andreas nodded to the bag. "It's yours now, Elizabeth."

Liz stood up, feeling weak at the knees. She took a few paces over to the bag, carefully opened it and then pulled the book out. As she did, a wave of emotion swept over her. This book would be just like the one that had been left for her. The one she'd never had a chance to see. And after all these years...

"Thank you, Andreas."

. . .

A short distance from the motel, Jay found Portia sitting on a fence stump with her guitar. Before her, a dusty plain stretched into the distance under the afternoon sun.

"Hey."

Portia turned round as Jay sat beside her. "Hi."

"Nice view."

Portia shrugged. "It has a certain charm. But to be honest, I just wanted to get outside."

"Yeah, I hear that," Jay replied. "I'm not too keen on staying in my motel room either."

"It's not that," Portia told him. "Although that *is* a big part of it. I'm just tired of being cooped up in general. Since Ivana, staying with my Mom and not being allowed to go out... It's like being locked up in a safe house or being in the witness protection program."

"You and me both," Jay agreed. "But remember, she's just trying to look after us."

Portia sighed. "I know. But you're staying voluntarily. What did *I* do to deserve this?"

"You're the daughter of a vampire hunter," Jay told her, giving her a smile. "And you know, that's kind of cool when you think about it."

"No, Jay. It's not cool. It's really not cool."

"All right," Jay said, waving one hand in a placating gesture. "I was just trying to cheer you up."

Portia stared at the plain. "I know. It's just this has been a pretty tough week for me. For *us*. And now that we're out of Palm Beach where this…" She found to her surprise that she couldn't say Hasheeba's name easily and ended up falling back on her mother's habit. "… where *she* can't find us, I think it's time to take a breather. To get outside and just forget about vampires for a while."

"There's one back at the motel," Jay reminded her.

"Well, apart from Andreas at any rate."

Jay was quiet for a moment. "Your mom seems to know Andreas pretty well."

"Not well," Portia told him. "They've only met once before. In World War I apparently."

Jay shook his head. "You know, I think finding out Liz is over three hundred years old is the hardest thing I've had to deal with all week. I just can't get my head around it."

"Me neither," Portia murmured.

"So…" Jay searched for another topic. "Any idea what your mom's plan is now? Apart from lying low?"

Portia shook her head. "I think lying low *is* the plan."

"So do we expect this Ha… Are we just waiting for this queen vampire to get bored and go back to Europe or wherever she came from?"

Portia frowned. "Well, what do you suggest we do?"

"Well, I don't know what you and your mom should do but I want to go back and help Matt. He's hanging out with this Cassandra and he's got no idea how much danger he's in."

Portia cast her gaze down. "Matt's my friend too, you know. But you can't go back to Palm Beach. *She's* probably there by now and she's looking for us. And that includes you."

Jay let out a breath in frustration. "But I feel so useless just sitting here."

"You're not useless," Portia told him, putting her hand on his. "You're here. And I don't know why but having you here in our little family of social outcasts... It makes me feel a little less crazy."

"Thanks." Jay smiled and turned to her. "But for the record, I don't think you and Liz are social outcasts. Your family's a little different from most but you're still a family. You love each other and care about each other. And that's pretty special. I mean, me... My parents are divorced. My dad's a serial womanizer and my mom drinks so much it's like she's not even on the planet. If I had the choice, I'd much rather be in your shoes."

"Even with all of this stuff?"

Jay nodded. "Even with all of this, yeah." He squeezed her hand. "I'm glad to be part of your life, Portia."

A few tears came to Portia's eyes and she found herself squeezing his hand back.

Jay let go and put his arm around her. She leaned into him and for a little while, they watched the view, ignoring the inherent discomfort in sitting on fence stumps for so long.

"Hey," Jay said after a little while, nodding to Portia's guitar. "Would you like to play a song? I'd love to hear one."

Portia looked at him in surprise and then down at the guitar. She'd almost forgotten about it but she'd brought it out of the motel room in order to play it. Her mind went back to when Ivana had asked her to play a song and it had felt strange then... While she'd wanted to please Ivana, she now knew her feelings had not entirely been her own. But with Jay, it was different.

With a smile on her lips, she put her left hand around the fretboard and started strumming a few chords with her right. Then she started to sing the same song she'd played for Ivana. *When you look my way*. She wasn't sure why she'd gone with that choice but somehow, it felt like the right one. It didn't feel like it had when she'd played it for Ivana or even when she'd written it in high school. As she played her song out there in the middle of nowhere with Jay beside her, it felt real.

When they got back to the motel, Portia thought she'd better check in on her mother. Jay meanwhile went to his room to watch TV with Kyle with a tentative arrangement for everyone to meet up again in a couple of hours for an early dinner. No going out after sunset.

Inside her room, Portia found her mother sitting on the sofa poring over an old book.

"What's that?" she asked her.

Liz looked up and Portia wondered what was wrong. In that moment, she saw so much in her mother's gaze. Love, grief, pride, regret...

"Close the door, honey," Liz said at last. "We have to talk."

Feeling a wave of apprehension, Portia did so and sat at the other end of the sofa. She waited for her mother to begin until she realized she was sitting frozen.

"Mom?"

Liz drew in a breath and let it out before gazing at her daughter. "I've failed you, Portia. I've completely and utterly failed you."

Portia reached over to her. "No, it's all right. Listen, Mom—"

Liz shook her head. "No, you don't understand. All your life, I've tried to shield you from all this. And now it's here and I've left you completely unprepared."

"Unprepared for what?"

Liz grimaced as she replied. "*Hasheeba*"—she spat the name out in disgust—"isn't here for me."

Portia guessed what her mom would say next but even so, the words struck her hard.

"She's here for you."

"Wild storms continue to lash the western seaboard today as..."

Kyle looked across from the kitchen at the stock news footage on the TV of waves crashing against piers and then his gaze wandered to his roommate on the sofa. The young man he'd seen at the beginning of the week—shell-shocked at the scene of a murder—now a fellow member of this strange but close-knit family that had taken him in last night after he'd lost everyone else close to him.

It was hard to believe they were all gone. Chief Hardgrave. Dave. Reeds. He felt a lump in his throat as he saw Alex again, sitting beside him with a plastic coffee cup in his hand. Joking. Making fun on occasions. But working by his side, supporting him and, in the end, taking that leap of faith to see with his own eyes whether or not vampires were real. And paying for it with his life.

Kyle pressed his lips together and took several slow breaths to compose himself. To bring him back to the here and now. Hiding out in a motel in the desert because some ancient, almost mythical creature was hunting his new family down.

He tried again to clear his thoughts. These were hardly better than his previous ones.

"Hey, Jay," he said, putting as much good cheer into his voice as he could manage. And doing pretty well. "Do you want a coffee or something?"

Jay turned around. "No, thanks. I'm okay at the moment."

As he went back to watching the TV, Kyle thought he had to hand it to the kid. Jay probably felt more awkward about the living arrangements than he did. He turned on the stove to boil some water. In the background, a news bulletin was running.

"Hey, Kyle."

Kyle froze as he heard the change in Jay's voice. The kid sounded like he'd just seen a ghost. And given all the run-ins they'd had with vampires this week, this was probable cause for alarm.

He frowned. "What is it?"

"You might want to take a look at this."

When Kyle turned around and saw what Jay was watching, he nearly turned white himself. There, on the TV was a picture of himself.

For a moment, he was speechless. Utterly. But mustering some inner strength, he found his voice. "Turn it up, Jay."

As Jay did, he started to catch what the newsreader was saying.

"... a massive manhunt that is currently underway for Lieutenant Kyle Destri of the Palm Beach Police Precinct. At present, Lieutenant Destri is the prime suspect in the deaths of eleven of his fellow police officers. Reports of what occurred last night have began to surface and while it is unclear exactly how it all happened, the authorities..."

Feeling his legs giving way beneath him, Kyle sat down and put his hands on his knees. Jay came over, gazing at him with equal measures of concern and sympathy. "Hey. That's just a big misunderstanding. We know that. I can vouch for you if anyone asks. When this blows over—"

Kyle waved him back. "No, Jay. Just give me a minute, will you?" He took a few deep breaths and found they didn't do much to help. "I think I'm going to be sick."

Liz waved her hand to the open book on the sofa beside her. "It's all here," she told her daughter, sighing. "Andreas was right. I was called to you. It wasn't a coincidence."

Considering the little time Portia had had to come to terms with all this, she took it remarkably well. "So it's destiny," she said, looking down. "No choice."

Liz climbed to her feet. A fierce determination had just come over her. "Well, it may be destiny. But I'll be damned if you have no choice."

Portia glanced up at this and did the last thing Liz expected. She laughed.

Liz gave her a quizzical look. "What's so funny?"

"You," Portia chuckled, still smiling. "That was almost American. You should try it with the accent." She sat up and tried a voice like the cowboys and gunslingers in the old westerns. "I'll be *damned* if you have no choice."

For several moments, Liz was at a loss as to what to say. Then, as the absurdity of it sank in, she laughed too. And as she felt a little of her tension draining away, she realized just how much she had built up this past week. It felt good to unwind, even if it was just for a minute.

"So what do we do now?" Portia asked once they'd both blown off some metaphorical steam.

The moment of levity past, List brought herself back to the present. "I'm not sure," she admitted.

"But I defeat her though, right?" Portia said. She put on a brave smile for her mother. "*Has—Hasheeba*. She prophesized it. Well, at least that's what Andreas said. Maybe we don't need to worry."

Liz shook her head. She wasn't so easily assured. "No. Look, I don't know that much about prophecies. I've heard it before that Hasheeba can sometimes see the future but I've never witnessed a firsthand demonstration for myself. However, if prophecies are indeed real, then I don't think people can just sit back like stoics and wait for them to actualize. Do you think you can just sit on a balcony, wait for Hasheeba to show up and then just inadvertently stake her?"

"Maybe not," Portia replied. "I wasn't suggesting that. But *maybe* I don't need a lifetime of training to be able to hold my own against her. I mean, how long did it take you to get that accurate with a crossbow?"

Liz thought about it. Her daughter probably wasn't going to like this. "About five or six years," she told her. "I didn't just start hunting vampires as soon as I became immortal."

"All right," Portia conceded. "Maybe I won't master the crossbow in the next few days." She frowned and gave Liz a funny look. "I don't get it. You had to go out and train for years to use that crossbow so you didn't get eagle eyes and a steady hand overnight. You don't have super strength. What's the point? What exactly does being a guardian do for you ? You're given immortality, okay, and you can recognize vampires... But is that it? Surely there's got to be more, right?" She reached for the book. "I mean, what else is in here?"

"Well, I don't know what you hope to find in that," Liz said, making no effort to stop her from flipping through it. After all, whoever had left it in Seville had left it for her. "But if you're looking for the secret of super strength, you're going to be disappointed."

Portia turned the pages with care. Liz was pleased to see she had the right amount of reverence for such an old text. "So what are all these pages filled up with? And how can I read it?"

Liz curled her lip. "Maybe somebody should transcribe the whole thing into modern English someday. Maybe I'll do it myself if we get through this weekend."

Portia looked up, the book momentarily forgotten. "What do you mean?"

Liz tried to wave the question away. "Nothing," she said, with a little shake of her head. "Anyway, if you want to know what most of that's filled up with, there's a lot of information on the code that guardians should follow, along with years of research on vampires. There are histories of the more prominent ones. Edward the Kinslayer has an entry. Even Andreas is in there, I found. There's also a number of pages written about how to—"

Portia winced. "No. Just wait. About what you said, I thought we were here to lie low for a while. The way you were talking the other night, I thought we might be out here for months. Maybe a year. Or I thought maybe we'd be moving from town to town and living off the grid." She shook her head in exasperation. "But we're not, *are we?* A small town. Not too many people to endanger. Open space where you can see someone coming for miles. This motel like a little fort in the middle of it. This isn't lying low. This is fortifying a position. It's a last stand." When Liz didn't reply, Portia looked her in the eyes. "Tell me I'm wrong, Mom."

Liz opened her mouth to reply when there was a knock at the door. She got up and patted Portia's shoulder as she passed her. "You're not wrong, honey. But it looks like this'll have to wait." She opened the door to see Kyle. Jay was standing behind him.

"What's wrong?"

"I just saw my face on national TV," Kyle told her, coming in. "I'm the prime suspect in the murder of all my fellow officers at the Palm Beach police station."

Liz stepped back and guided him past her daughter, sitting him on the sofa. He looked like he could barely stand. Jay came inside and without a word, held Portia's hand. Portia squeezed it in return. Liz for her part didn't notice the gesture. Her gaze was on Kyle.

"It's because I came out here with you," Kyle said, looking at her with despair in his eyes. "They think I ran because I'm guilty."

There was an accusation there, Liz knew, but she knew better than to take it personally. Kyle was confused and upset. The world he'd built for himself over many years had just crumbled around him.

"It wouldn't have made a difference if you stayed," she told him. "Except you'd be in police custody right now. They don't think you did it because you ran. They think you did it because they're under Hasheeba's influence." It was funny, Liz noticed absently. It seemed now the more she said the woman's name, the easier it was. Perhaps it was a good omen.

"And how do you figure that?" Kyle asked her.

"Because," Liz replied, "she did the exact same thing to me three hundred years ago. Remember?"

Kyle's demeanor changed at once. He remembered.

Liz kept going. "A town full of people—good people who I'd known all my life—were ready to lynch me or burn me alive because Hasheeba had swayed them. She could turn you too if she ever set her eyes on you. That's what makes her so much more dangerous than other vampires. She doesn't just kill. She corrupts."

Kyle looked down and shook his head. "I'm sorry. I never meant to—"

"You never meant any of this to happen?" At this, Liz snapped. "I warned you to let me handle it but, no, you wanted to see vampires with your own eyes. Well, congratulations. You've seen them. You practically invited them into your life." She let out a sigh. "I'm sorry about your colleagues. And I'm sorry this thing in the news has happened. But this is what vampires bring. This is what I try to protect people from. You. Jay. Portia. Apart from a select few like Andreas, they're bad news."

Looking up again, Kyle's expression and manner were now subdued and there was a look of remorse in his gaze. "You're right. I've only got myself to blame. And, I suppose, the authorities are right too. I might not have intended it but *I* was the one who got my friends and colleagues killed when I brought Eddie and Cassandra into the station." He climbed to his feet, as though he'd discovered hidden reserves of strength. "But I'm here now, for better or worse. And since I can't go home, I may as well try to make myself useful. So if there's anything I can do to help you, I'm entirely at your service."

"Me too," Jay chimed in.

Liz glanced back and saw him holding her daughter's hand. She pressed her lips together in a tight smile.

"All right," she said. "Since we're all in harm's way already. Hasheeba is coming here. According to Andreas, she had a vision of some kind and now she believes Portia is going to destroy her. That's why Ivana tried to turn her. And that's why Edward the Kinslayer and Cassandra were here. That's why she's coming too. Now, whether or not she really had this vision or if there's any truth in it, there's no time for you, Portia, to train yourself to face her."

She caught her daughter's eye and Portia nodded. She understood the reality of the situation.

"I have to kill Hasheeba," Liz said. She went to a cupboard in the kitchen and pulled out some vaguely familiar items. No one else in the room had seen them up close yet but they knew a crossbow when they saw one. And a sharpened shaft of wood was a rather easy thing to recognize as well. "I only need one good shot," she continued. "It doesn't matter whether a vampire is thirty years old or eight hundred. And regardless of how strong they are after sunset, they're still heir to the thousand natural shocks that we are. Most injuries that are fatal to us will incapacitate them. And losing their head or getting pierced through the heart with a sharp piece of wood will kill them."

"And what about this motel?" Kyle asked. "Are we safe here?"

"No vampire can come in uninvited," Liz told him. "If that's what you mean. But remember, Edward couldn't enter your car uninvited either but that didn't stop him from almost killing you. These vampires aren't stupid. And Hasheeba will be more cunning than the oldest ones I've ever faced."

Jay raised a tentative hand. "Hang on a minute though. I thought Hash... I thought Ha... I thought she couldn't find us here."

"She'll find us," Liz replied. "We've just bought some time. That's all." She gave Portia a knowing glance. "And we can fortify our position here. We've got good visibility in most directions..." She paused as a thought occurred to her. "And you know what? I've just thought of something you and Kyle can do, Jay. How'd you like to be lookouts?"

A short walk from the Palm Beach dock, Cassandra looked at the creature scratching at the dirt and making quiet grunts and snarls. Human in shape but so haggard and scrawny... with skin so pallid it was almost gray. Its prominent sharp teeth suited its beastly appearance, as did its tattered, dirty gray clothes and the rattling chain around its neck. It was appalling.

She looked up at the ancient goddess holding the chain's end, radiant with beauty after they had drunk their fill... and left Matt lying in that motel room.

She tried to banish the memory from her mind. How many other young men had she drunk from over the years? She hadn't been troubled by them. But then, she hadn't grown tired of Edward in those days. Was that it? Or was it something else?

"Something troubles you, my dear?" Hasheeba asked.

Cassandra looked up and shook her head, feeling some of her pain fading away. "No." Her eyes then fell on the disgusting creature crawling around at her mistress's feet and she scowled. "And yes. What *is* that thing?"

Hasheeba smiled. She'd been quite tight lipped about it since she'd taken it out of the crate where it had spent the past god-knows-how-many months on its journey to the states. "You don't like it?"

Cassandra was unable to hide her distaste at the very sight of it. "It's hideous. And it smells like rotten meat."

"Well, we only need it for a short time," Hasheeba assured her. "Then we can put it out of its misery. But as for what it is, I'm surprised you can't guess. Because there but for the grace of God, go us. It's a feral vampire. The creature never had a chance. It was probably not that smart as a human and once it was turned, its lust for blood overcame all its senses. I usually put them down whenever I see them—and I'll kill any vampire on sight if I find out they've created one—but occasionally I'll keep them alive for a while. They have their uses and with a little patience, they can be trained."

"It's a tracker?"

"Very good."

Cassandra frowned. "But don't we need a scent for it to follow? We don't have anything belonging to Elizabeth for it to use."

"No," Hasheeba agreed, pulling out a bloodied cloth from a fold in her dress. "But I found a little of Andreas' blood at the crime scene you and Edward created last night. And if I can find our wayward kinsman, we can find Elizabeth. And the girl." She put it away.

Cassandra shuddered as she opened the back of the van they'd stolen. The deformed grotesque at Hasheeba's feet almost leapt with excitement at the sight of the van's driver lying inside.

"You're not going to let it... *eat* in the van, are you?" she asked.

Hasheeba pursed her lips. "No. We don't want that." She scanned the street for somewhere more suitable then handed the chain to Cassandra. "Here. Take it and its meal and feed it behind the dumpster. Then clean up the body." She smiled. "We don't want to leave another crime scene for the nice young police officers we met today."

Right then, Cassandra could think of nothing she'd like less than feeding this animal but in Hasheeba's power, she was helpless to do anything but obey her every whim. Suppressing any outward sign of reluctance, she started her chores.

Liz frowned as she flipped through the book Andreas had given her. There were several distinct handwriting styles used throughout, as well as different languages— some she knew and others she didn't—and as for the content...

It didn't seem as though anyone had taken the time to sit down, categorize and index all the notes left by guardians over the centuries and write the definitive textbook on 'How to be a Guardian'.

She scoured the pages looking for references to Hasheeba and found some. But there were so many pages, she knew she'd have to read the whole thing one day in order to find them all. Maybe *she'd* write the definitive textbook one day and do all her successors a favor...

Her successors.

She closed the book and opened it again at the page that Andreas had bookmarked for her. And for the second time, she read the section explaining how guardians passed their immortality onto others. The secret that appeared so simple.

To pass your immortality to another, all you must do is wish it.

She shut the book. Andreas had found it written elsewhere in the book, in older forms of English and some of those other languages but it was always the same thing.

She shook her head. It wasn't simple. Knowing what it was like, how could she *wish* her immortality on someone else? Especially her own daughter?

She put the question aside. There was no point in dwelling on it now.

Trying a new page at random, she found another reference to Hasheeba.

And t hath seemed as though through nay oth'r means but h'r shall, the sky did turn black and wast anon with lightning t'rn asund'r.

This was an older reference. Written in Elizabethan English. Her language.

'And it seemed as though through no other means but her will, the sky turned black and was soon with lightning torn asunder.'

Liz opened Andreas' door and stepped inside. Andreas was where she'd left him, still lying on the sofa.

"How are you feeling?" she asked.

Andreas stretched his arms out and, to Liz's surprise pulled himself into an upright position. "A little better, I think."

"Yeah, well," Liz said quickly, "don't go straining yourself too quickly."

Andreas nodded. "I'll try to take it easy. How did Portia take it?"

Liz shrugged, sitting beside him. "About as well as could be expected. Actually, she was pretty remarkable about it really."

"That's good."

"Yeah." Liz was quiet for a moment. "Andreas. There's something I want to ask you. Have you ever met Hasheeba?"

A little of Andreas' color drained from his face. "Once," he said. "In Crete. It was 1869. Late July."

"You remember the month?"

"I remember the date," Andreas told her. "The 24th. I met Cassandra that day as well. She was... She was in Hasheeba's employ, so to speak."

"Was Edward there too?"

Andreas shook his head. "No. I hadn't met him yet."

"So what happened?"

"When I met Cassandra, I thought she was like me," Andreas said. "A kindred spirit. Someone who hadn't let the blood lust turn them into a monster. She befriended me and took me to this incredible villa to meet her dame, as she described her."

"Hasheeba?"

Andreas nodded again. "Right."

"What was she like?"

Some of Andreas' color returned, though mostly in a reddening of the cheeks. "Actually, now that you're asking me, it's a little embarrassing to talk about it."

"Please," Liz insisted.

"Well," Andreas said, giving in with a sigh, "she was breathtaking. And it felt as though I'd fallen in love with her from the moment I saw her. Then when she invited me to her bed chamber, I couldn't think of anything I'd ever desired more. It was..."

Liz relented a little this time and gave him an understanding smile. "All right. I can see how this might be a little awkward."

"A *little*?"

"Okay," Liz conceded. "Very. So how can I put this delicately? There was copulation involved here?"

"Not quite," Andreas confessed, looking as though he wished he'd never started his tale. "Hasheeba offered herself to me but not without something in return first. She wanted me to drink her blood."

Liz frowned. "But you were already a vampire. What would drinking her blood do to you?"

"I know," Andreas said. "It seems kind of pointless. But I don't think it was. I think if I had given in to her offer, I would have become like her. I would have lost what was left of my humanity."

This satisfied Liz to an extent but not completely. "But why would she want to do that? Was she looking for a companion to be with her forever?"

Andreas cast his gaze down and a faint smile crossed his lips. "Maybe. But somehow, I don't think so. I think she probably just thought it was good sport."

"Hm. And you say you didn't give in. You didn't drink at all?"

Andreas looked up. "I ran."

Liz studied his face, searching for any sign of a lie. "And you escaped? Just like that?"

"I had a little bit of the element of surprise," he explained. "And the villa had enough corridors to give me some cover. Plus, Cassandra distracted her when she knew what was going on, telling her I'd gone one way when I'd gone the other."

Again, Liz wasn't entirely satisfied with the account. "Why would Cassandra help you?"

"She pulled Edward off me last night," Andreas pointed out. "She hasn't entirely lost her better nature."

"That's something," Liz said, a pensive gaze in her eyes. "Actually, it's a big thing. And if she's the only other vampire working with Hasheeba here, that could be useful. If she's turned away from her before..."

"Yes," Andreas agreed.

"Still, it seems strange that Hasheeba lost you so easily once you were out of her sight. Wouldn't she—I don't know—*sense* you?

Andreas shrugged. "I may be a vampire but I'm not as old as she is. I don't know what she's capable of any more than you do. But when you say I got away from her easily, that's not true. The whole time I was running, I had this yearning to go back to her that was so strong it hurt. Even after I'd left Crete, it hurt. For years. Cassandra felt it too when she left. And maybe that's her real power. She'll take everything from you if she can and, in return, you'll love her."

· · ·

214

When Liz went out onto the balcony, the evening air was noticeably cooler than the heat of the day. It was pleasant and she wished she could just put a chair outside and enjoy it. But tonight, they had to be on their guard. And soon, they'd begin their rotating shifts.

She saw Kyle leaning on the rail, gazing at the now gray landscape stretching into the distance.

"Twenty times stronger after sunset?" he wondered aloud, his voice soft.

Liz came alongside him. "Well, no one's ever run tests on a vampire in a lab to check the figure. But you've seen what they can do."

The memory of Eddie snapping Alex like a toothpick came back to Kyle, as clear as though he were right back in the station. "True," he murmured.

Liz squeezed his hand.

"Do you think she'll come tonight?" he asked her.

Liz took in a breath of the cooler evening air. The stars were brilliant here, away from the lights of Palm Beach. Although they disappeared in darkness on the western horizon. Heavy clouds according to the weather forecast and they were drifting their way. Occasional sparks and flashes, minute in appearance to her, lit the clouds up. But they were still very distant. Very faint.

"I don't think so," she told him. "She's probably not that far away now but I doubt even she could find us this quickly."

"Should we hide the cars?" Kyle suggested.

Liz let go of his hand. "I think it's a bit too late for that. Besides, we might need them."

"Or if she doesn't show up tonight, what if we leave in the morning and try to go—"

"Where?" Liz asked, cutting him off. "You're a wanted man, remember? Besides, I don't want to hide any more. I've been hiding from her for three hundred years now. It's long enough."

"But what about Portia?"

Liz sighed. "I've thought about her too. Believe me."

A pair of headlights appeared in the far distance and they watched as the car approached. It turned off the main road at the gas station and a few minutes later, crawled into the parking lot below.

Liz and Kyle watched as the doors opened and a small family climbed out. Kyle breathed a sigh of relief and turned to Liz. "Fellow lodgers."

"Yeah, it looks like it," Liz agreed. She turned away from the balcony and gave him a nudge. "You'd better get indoors for a bit. They might recognize you from the news."

Kyle nodded, his smile gone in a moment. "What are we going to do about that?"

"I don't know yet," Liz said, opening her door. "But we'll think of something. Do you want to come in with me for a little while? Jay's all right. He and Portia are watching a DVD he bought. Maybe we can have a cup of tea. Or a coffee if it's more your taste."

Kyle shrugged. "Tea's nice. I like tea."

Liz smiled as she let him in. "You like *me*. That's what you mean. I knew it when we were at the cafe the other day." She closed the door behind him. "But that's all right. I like me too. And"—she patted him on the shoulder—"despite your stubbornness in not listening to me earlier, I like you too."

A smile crossed Kyle's lips again as well but it faded as they came into the kitchen and a pensive mood came over him.

"I lost my parents when I was six years old," he told Liz as she put the pot on. When she looked back, he hurried on. "They weren't killed by vampires. It was a hit and run. Some guy high on half a dozen different types of drugs and he'd just robbed a convenience store. Just plowed right into them when he lost control of the vehicle and got another eighty yards before he crashed."

Liz looked at him with sympathy. "I'm sorry."

Kyle shrugged. "It was a long time ago now. But that's what made me want to be a cop. After they died though, I stayed in an orphanage for a few years until a foster family took me in. And there was a girl I liked there. She was much older than I was—well, not as old as you, of course—and she was a little bit of a rebel. She was kind to all of us though and I used to think that meant she liked me…" He broke off here, looking a bit embarrassed. "Well, you know how it is."

Liz nodded. "I think I understand."

"But she didn't want to be taken in by anyone. It was like being an orphan was a badge of honor and a foster family would take that away. I often told her I felt the same way but that was mostly because I had a bit of a crush on her." He stopped his tale abruptly. "And one day"—he struggled to get the words out, almost choking on them—"she was gone." He cleared his throat and rubbed tears from his eyes. "Sorry."

"Don't be," Liz interjected, placing her hand on his shoulder. "She was murdered?"

Kyle nodded, composing himself. "Yeah."

"Vampire?"

Kyle nodded again and sat down at the counter.

"How old were you?" Liz asked.

"I was eleven."

Now Liz understood where all of this had been going. "So this obsession goes back to when you were a kid then?"

"Before I ever joined the police," Kyle told her. "I was never enamored with vampires, Liz. I wanted to find them and show them that they're not above us. That we can fight back."

"They're not above us," Liz assured him. "Their strength. Their longevity. This makes them different but it doesn't make them better. Is some steroid-using thug on PCP better than you? Is an eighty-year old man who had everything in life handed to him on a plate, who never learned to take responsibility for anything, better than a bright young kid with a dream of making the world a better place?"

"No, I guess not," Kyle conceded.

"We don't need to prove anything to vampires," Liz told him. "Or to ourselves. And you know, while I hunt them, I don't wander the world looking for them. I move around a bit, sure. But mostly I just keep my eye open. This week, in case you haven't realized, isn't a typical week for me."

"Yeah," Kyle said. "I figured that. And actually, I think I've figured you out too."

Liz was getting some mugs out of the cupboard. "Me?"

"You're right. You're not out there trying to hunt down every last vampire on the planet. You're just trying to protect people. Clearly, you've been trying to protect Portia all her life. And this week, you've also been trying to protect me."

"You say that like it's a bad thing."

Kyle frowned, hesitating before he spoke. "Well, it's not necessarily a bad thing. But I think it *could* be. Sometimes people don't want to be protected."

"Well," Liz said as she made the tea, "maybe that's true. But if I hadn't been protecting my daughter, she'd be a vampire now. And if Andreas or I hadn't come when Edward was trying to kill you, we wouldn't be talking now."

"I agree," Kyle said. "But Portia's going to have to stand on her own one day, right? You can't hold her back and keep her from the outside world. And I may not be three hundred but I like to be able to stand on my own two feet as well sometimes. Even if I fall occasionally. But I also think..." Here he hesitated. "I think you try to protect *yourself* a little bit too much from people. That day at the cafe, I thought we'd made a connection but then you pushed me away. And I wasn't trying to be your boyfriend or anything. I just thought that maybe we could be friends."

"You say that," Liz told him, bringing over the mugs and getting some milk from the fridge. She didn't offer him any sugar on account of the fact that there wasn't any. "But I think you wanted more. Trust me, when you've been around as long as I have, you get to know the signals."

"Okay," Kyle said, pouring some milk in his mug and putting it back down. "Thanks for the tea, by the way."

Liz smiled. "It's all right. Go on."

"I was just going to say you're right."

"Of course I am," Liz replied, feigning surprise that he'd even think it could be otherwise.

"But, even so," Kyle continued, "is that such a bad thing? That I like you? That I want to know you better? I mean, what's wrong with that? Is it because you're immortal?"

Liz sighed. "Kyle, you *know* it's because I'm immortal. It can't work."

"But why not?"

"Because it would end in grief. You know that too."

"You're right," Kyle said. "I do. But so does all life really, when you think of it. But does that mean we shouldn't allow ourselves to find happiness wherever we can? I mean, what about you and Portia? There's grief there too, at the end. Maybe not in the next few years. But eventually, your own daughter is going to grow older than you. But you've had many happy years together, right? And you'll have many more. What's different?"

"Nothing's different," Liz retorted with sudden heat. To her irritation, her eyes were moist with tears. "But I came across Portia by chance. I never tried to have a daughter of my own. Or a lover. I've lost so many people in my life. Family. Friends. I don't want to lose more."

"But what's the alternative?" Kyle asked. "An eternity alone? We could make it work for a while at least. Years.

And afterward, *those* years could be happy memories for years more to come."

Liz finished her cup of tea in one gulp and got up. "I'm going back to keep my eye out. Maybe you and Jay can take over for a few hours after his movie's finished and then I can relieve you later on."

She opened the door and closed it again before Kyle could say anything else. He was right, she knew. And that was the thing that upset her the most.

It was quiet again outside, although she heard the muffled noise a few doors down of the family that had just piled out of their car. She glanced in that direction when the door next to hers opened and Andreas stepped out.

"Hi, Elizabeth."

She smiled. "You can call me Liz if you want, you know. Everyone else does."

"That's how they know you," Andreas replied. "But it's not how I remember you. I see you and I'm brought right back to that day in 1915. It's hard to even believe we're not in uniform."

"I'd imagine that's not on your list of fond memories."

"Oddly enough," Andreas confessed, "it's always been a memory I've held close. One of the few times I've felt connected to the world and the people around me. And I think this time will be another one."

"So you'll fondly reminisce about these past few days in the future as well then?"

"I hope so." Andreas gave her a nod and started walking down the balcony.

"Where are you going?" she asked him. She noticed he had his backpack with him.

"I'm checking the perimeter," Andreas told her, glancing back over his shoulder. "So to speak."

"But your injury—"

"It's all right. I've been lying in bed long enough."

Liz pursed her lips. His injury this time wasn't anywhere near as severe as what he had suffered in the trenches and her experience in nursing injured vampires back to health was limited to only these two cases. Maybe he was fine. Also, as she watched him leaving, she thought about what Kyle had told her about protecting people too much... and Andreas was definitely old enough to take care of himself.

"Be careful," she called after him.

"I will," he replied as he reached the stairs at the end of the balcony. "Don't wait up for me."

When he was gone, it was very quiet. The new arrivals several doors down sounded like they'd already turned in. And if they'd had a long day on the road, that was pretty reasonable. Actually, Liz thought, even if they hadn't had a long day, turning in early made sense. It wasn't as though there was much to do around here.

Aside from keeping a lookout for the oldest known vampire in existence.

She sighed and watched the progress of the storm. It was still quite far off but definitely closer than before.

...the sky did turn black and wast anon with lightning t'rn asund'r.

She wondered what the weather bureau made of it.

Portia opened another page of the book. It wasn't ideal bedtime reading but the way some of these guardians rambled on, it was certainly making her sleepy. Besides, if she was supposed to follow in her mom's footsteps, it seemed to her she ought to make some effort to familiarize herself with this stuff.

She blinked a few times to moisten her eyes and had a look at the page she'd turned to.

And it seems to me that in her desire to conquer the desires of others, the blood of one who goes willingly to her without resisting would be like poison in her veins.

Portia re-read the sentence, then flipped to the previous page. It was as she'd thought. She'd found a reference to Hasheeba.

She wondered why none of the various guardians over the years had got around to staking her. Why her mom hadn't. Was the fact that everyone else had failed to deal with Hasheeba related to the vampire's own vision of her demise? That she, Portia, was the one destined to do the deed?

She thought about her mother's crossbow and how it'd take years to master it to a point where she could use it accurately enough to take down a swift moving vampire. And how, without some means of propelling a wooden stake with sufficient force, she'd have no chance of actually driving it through Hasheeba's heart by hand.

And somehow, she doubted Hasheeba would lie still long enough for her to drive a stake into her with a mallet like people did in some of the old stories.

So just what was she of all people supposed to do to bring down the most powerful vampire in existence?

With a sigh, she turned the page over and, for the third time, read the phrase that had arrested her attention.

...the blood of one who goes willingly to her without resisting would be like poison in her veins.

Was there anything in that, she wondered, or was it just the philosophical ramblings of someone who'd been a better poet than a guardian? She slid a piece of paper in to mark the spot and shut the book.

Its headlights off, the van followed the lonely road at a modest speed. Through the open rear window, a vile deformed face sniffed the air and began to growl. The van stopped.

"There are lights ahead," Cassandra said, sitting in the driver's seat. "On the right."

Her passenger nodded. "We will investigate soon enough. But let our pet out for a moment."

Cassandra was all too familiar with this routine. More walking around with this revolting fiend on the end of a chain, while her mistress sat back and smiled with closed eyes. She turned to her right out of curiosity and sure enough, Hasheeba had already adopted the pose. Though whether she was sleeping or simply waiting, Cassandra couldn't tell.

Suppressing a sigh, she climbed out of the van and fetched Hasheeba's pet. It headed away from the road and—to her surprise—in the opposite direction of the lights. It led her over dry grass and occasional patches of sand. They came across a wire fence and in her impatience, Cassandra kicked a stump down so she didn't have to climb over it. As Hasheeba's pet scrambled past, it tangled one of its legs in wire. Cassandra laughed at it and let it drag the wire a few hundred feet before it came free by itself.

"Stupid creature," she muttered.

It then began to get excited, running in circles and growling more and more. Cassandra frowned, wondering what had come over it. She looked around but there wasn't much to see. Just a couple of small hills, basking in the occasional flashes of the storm that had followed her and Hasheeba from Palm Beach. Was there something behind one of them?

She moved closer and a dark figure leapt out, running straight past her and grappling with Hasheeba's pet. Rolling it onto its back and holding it down with one hand, he gripped a wooden stake with the other and brought it down. The creature let out a strangled cry of pain and after a couple of spasms, it lay still.

Cassandra realized she hadn't moved a muscle to stop the man. She watched as he rose to his feet, while the remains of the creature crumbled into dust and blew away.

"Andreas," she said, recognizing her old acquaintance and, on occasions, friend.

"I thought Hasheeba might have someone doing her dirty work," he told her. "She's using you. Just as she used that thing"—he gestured to the spot where the creature had died, marked now only by the chain leash it had left behind—"and anything and anyone she can find."

"I know," Cassandra told him, feeling a sudden rush of emotion. "But you haven't been near her for many years."

"You lured me into her bed chambers once, in case you've forgotten," Andreas told her. "When you were working for her on Crete. I resisted her then. So did you in the end."

Cassandra sighed. "We resisted her together then. It's different now. She's stronger and I'm on my own. And when Edward was with me, he didn't resist her at all. That made it harder."

"Is she close?"

"She's in a van on the main road," Cassandra said. "She's waiting for me."

"And is she planning to kill Portia herself or has she left that job to you?"

"She hasn't told me what her plan is. I don't think she trusts me."

Nodding in reply, Andreas crouched down and unslung a backpack. He pulled out a short crossbow.

"Is that Elizabeth's?" Cassandra asked.

"Elizabeth isn't the only one with a crossbow," Andreas replied. "I got this from a guy who was hoarding weapons in his garage."

"And you killed him, I take it."

"He was a bad man."

Cassandra raised her eyebrows at this then shrugged. "Of course he was. You've always been the noble one."

Andreas ignored the remark as he loaded the crossbow. They'd been over this enough times before. "Are you coming?"

He appeared to be all swagger and confidence but Cassandra wasn't fooled. Blood was soaking through his shirt where Edward had injured him and now it trickled out of a dozen new cuts and gashes inflicted by Hasheeba's pet.

"She'll kill you," she told him.

"If you don't want to come, then don't come," he replied, though there was no impatience in his voice. And without waiting for a reply, he walked off in the direction of the road.

A peel of thunder crashed in the distance. Cassandra turned her gaze to the sky and shook her head. "This is stupid," she muttered. "I'm a vampire."

But so was Andreas. And Hasheeba was a bitch.

With a sigh, she set off for the road as well. "Wait up."

When they reached the road though, the van had disappeared. Cassandra looked both ways but it was nowhere in sight.

"She must have suspected something was wrong," she said. "Nothing gets by her."

There was a grim set to Andreas' gaze as he looked at the lights in the distance. "Maybe she didn't feel like waiting."

Cassandra followed his gaze. "Is Elizabeth there?"

Andreas nodded.

. . .

Portia stirred in her sheets. She wondered what had woken her.

"Portia." The voice was faint, like a whisper... No, Portia decided. It was more like a murmur in her ear. And the voice was familiar.

"Portia. I'm here. It's me."

She sat up and there, sitting on the end of her bed, was Ivana. Her heart swelled with joy and she reached out for her. "Ivana. I thought I'd lost you."

"I'm here," her companion assured her, brushing her hair and caressing her cheeks.

"But it's not safe here," Portia said. "My mom..." She turned to the bed next to her but... She blinked. The bed was gone. She was alone. And as her eyes grew accustomed to the dark, she realized she was in her own room again. Her own place.

With a sigh of relief, she leaned into Ivana's embrace.

"Yes," Ivana told her. "You're safe now. I'm here."

Sunday

It WAS RAINING OUTSIDE AND, BY THE SOUNDS of things, the wind had really picked up during the night. Liz had some jam on toast and made some tea as she wondered what the day had in store for everyone. The store... Maybe it was worth making another trip down there to see if they had anything they could use for tripwires, alarms or traps. Because today, in all likelihood, was going to be it. Or tonight rather. Somehow she doubted Hasheeba would approach before sunset when she wasn't at her strongest.

Although as she thought this, Liz wondered. Other vampires lost most of their strength during the day and were, for most intents and purposes, like regular people. But was the self-proclaimed queen of everything in existence like other vampires in this respect? After all, her abilities to control the minds of others went far beyond Ivana's ability to hold Portia silent against her will...

The train of thought came to a halt as Liz realized that Portia was being pretty silent right now as well.

She looked at the clock on the wall and saw it was a little after 8:30. It wasn't particularly late in the morning for Portia to still be in bed, and she wasn't planning to check on Kyle and Jay until after 9.00. But for some reason, she wondered. Maybe it was motherly instinct but she went into the room and found Portia looking quite pale. And when she put her hand on her cheek, it was cold. She touched her forehead next. That was hot. And it looked like Portia had sweated a lot during the night as well.

Liz gave her a gentle shake. "Portia, are you feeling all right?"

But Portia kept on sleeping.

She'd need some fluids if she was running a fever, Liz knew, but she decided to let her sleep a little longer. And right then, she had an alarming thought.

The quality of Sunday morning cartoons not being up to Jay's high standards of entertainment, he had put on a DVD he'd had in his car.

He sat with Kyle on the sofa, both of them with a mug of coffee in hand, and watched the mindless mayhem on the screen.

"This is pretty damn stupid," Kyle said in a manner of casual observation after a few minutes of car stunts and explosions.

Jay shrugged. "Yeah. But there's something soothing about switching your brain off for a couple of hours. Besides, we could always watch a vampire movie if you prefer."

Kyle rolled his eyes. "No, thanks."

For a few more minutes, they watched the antics of a maverick cop who let neither parked cars nor public infrastructure stand between him and the man he was after... until a knock on the door brought them back to the motel room.

Kyle opened it and Liz came in, looking pretty upset. "Did Portia leave her room last night?" she demanded.

Kyle exchanged a puzzled glance with Jay then looked back at Liz. "No, why?"

"Are you sure?" Liz asked. "Did you or Jay leave the balcony at any time or fall asleep?"

"We were awake the whole time," Kyle insisted, deciding to handle the talking for both of them while Jay stopped the movie. "Portia never left her room and no one came in."

Liz let out a breath. "All right then. What about Andreas? Did he come back last night?"

Kyle frowned. "No. He's not in his room?"

"No. I just checked. He went out last night to have a look around."

"Did he take a car?"

"No, he went on foot." Liz looked about as tense as Kyle had seen her. "Are you sure neither of you saw anything strange last night?"

"No," Kyle told her. "We were on the balcony until you came out and I was with you for a few hours after that. We didn't see anything. Liz, what's wrong?"

"She got to Portia. Somehow. It's like it was when Ivana was trying to turn her. She's drained and lethargic."

"But she wasn't here," Kyle said. "She couldn't have done anything. Are you sure Portia isn't just coming down with..." He broke off. Liz had dealt with vampires for three hundred years. She knew what she was talking about.

"What can I do?" he asked instead.

Liz shook her head. "I don't think you can help me during daylight hours. We can't risk anyone outside seeing you and bringing the police here." She looked at the other occupant in the room. "Jay, do you think you can go to the store and get a few things?" She paused as she realized the enormity of what she was really asking him. "You're the only one of us Hasheeba might not recognize."

By the color draining from Jay's face, he now had some concept of the enormity of the task as well. "She's here?"

"She's here," Liz told him. "And this is not a large town."

"And she *might* not recognize me, you say?"

Liz hesitated. "We don't know what she might have learned from Matt." She was quite certain now that Jay wouldn't be seeing his friend again.

Jay nodded and, as she looked at him, it seemed to Liz the carefree kid from her class a week ago was gone. And in his place was a young man.

"So these things you need," he said. "Are they for Portia?"

"Yes."

"Then I'll go and get them."

Liz squeezed his shoulder in gratitude. "Thanks, Jay. I need you to get a few bottles of those sports drinks with the electrolytes, and some ibuprofen."

Jay stared at her with a puzzled expression. "That's it?"

Liz gave him a little smile. "Portia doesn't need any garlic, Jay. Just some fluids and a good breakfast. I'll take care of the second item. You take care of the first. Oh, and there might be something else we can do too but I'm not sure yet. We can talk about it when you get back."

Once he left, Liz turned to the room's remaining occupant. "What's your blood type, Kyle?"

While Jay was getting sports drinks, Liz went back to her room, got a hand towel, filled a bowl with hot water and dabbed it on Portia's forehead until she came to. She appeared more than a little dazed as she sat up and looked around.

"What's this?" she asked, wiping droplets off her forehead and looking at the bowl and the towel in her mother's hand.

"You didn't look well," Liz told her. "And you weren't responsive when I tried to wake you up. How are you feeling, by the way? Have you got a fever? A chill?"

Portia thought about it. "I've got a headache. I don't know about the other things. But I do feel tired."

"Can you remember anything strange happening last night? Did you have any bad dreams or something?"

Portia bit her lip. "Not... bad dreams." She looked at her mother in concern. "But I had a dream about Ivana. It was... vivid."

"It felt real?"

Portia nodded. "Very."

Liz was quiet for a moment. "I think Hasheeba was here. Not physically in this room. But I think that was her in your dream. She reached out to you as Ivana."

Portia went a lighter shade of pale. "Why?"

"I'm not sure exactly but it seems like you're a lot weaker this morning and you're a bit disoriented. Maybe she's wearing you down so it's easier for her to deal with you."

"Are you sure you're not reaching here?" Portia asked. "How can she get inside my head?"

"She can influence minds, honey. You know that. We've seen enough examples of it."

"But she's never met me."

Liz fell quiet for a moment. "Wait a minute..."

"What ?"

"I'm just thinking. When Ivana tried to turn you, she drank your blood."

Portia grimaced. "Yeah, thanks Mom. That's just what I need to get over the experience. Reminders."

"No, bear with me." Liz's voice was firm. "Portia, I didn't ask you at the time because I didn't want to worry you but it's important now. Did you drink any of Ivana's blood?"

Portia made a face. "Did I drink her blood?"

"Just answer the question, honey. Did you? Do you remember what happened that night?"

Portia sighed. "I don't remember a lot of what happened. Between the time when I called you and when Jay showed up, it's all a bit hazy."

Liz nodded. "Then it sounds to me like you did. You're describing a trance-like state and that's what happens in these situations. Which means Ivana was a lot closer to turning you than I thought. And I was just thinking how vampires share a mental link with people they've turned... and people they're in the process of turning. Ivana definitely had a link with you. We both know that. But just now, it occured to me that this link could go further. That a vampire could have a link with the offspring of one of their own. You see, I don't know who made Ivana what she was but, now that I think about it, it's entirely possible it was Hasheeba. And she might well have turned Edward and Cassandra too. And if that's so, it might not be some random gang of vampires that she's sent our way this week. These creatures might be a family."

Portia sighed. "I'm really tired, Mom. So if they're a family, so what? What about it?"

"Well, if I'm right," Liz explained, "then Hasheeba might well have a connection to you through Ivana."

"So what does that make me?" Portia now sounded more annoyed by all of this than frightened. "Her grand-daughter?"

Picking up on the shift in her daughter's mood, Liz backed up a little. "I'm just trying to figure out what she's done to you."

However, it was too late. Teary eyed all of a sudden, Portia turned her head away. "Well, figure it out somewhere else!"

"Portia," Liz said, putting a hand on her shoulder. "I know how hard it is—"

"Do you?" Portia demanded, whirling on her. "I was starting college this year, Mom! I wanted to learn new things and meet people. I thought maybe I could meet some other musicians on campus and make a band. I was excited about it. And now we're hiding in a motel in the middle of the desert, possibly fugitives from the law because of what's happened with Kyle... and there's this thousand year-old bitch who's trying to kill me or make me into a vampire. And now it seems she can take either option without even entering the room. So yeah—it's hard, Mom. Thanks for telling me."

She turned away again and Liz got up. "I'm sorry, honey."

Just a few hundred feet from the motel, Jay felt like he was in enemy territory. There were only a handful of people around—locals, he assumed—but he found himself wary of each and every one of them. Were they under Hasheeba's influence? Were they all watching him behind his back?

He tried not to think about it.

The lady behind the counter in the store was friendly enough though. And the other customers smiled at him as he passed them. Maybe, he decided, he was getting himself worked up over nothing.

"Jay," a voice murmured from the other side of a shelf as he was about to leave.

Or, Jay decided, maybe he wasn't being so paranoid after all.

He peered around the corner. "Andreas?"

The vampire was there, sporting a whole host of new injuries.

"You look like hell," Jay told him, keeping his voice down. "What happened?"

"Long story," Andreas told him. "But you can relay a bit of it to Liz. Hasheeba's here. Not in this store" —he added this when Jay started looking in every direction— "but she's close by. Cassandra was with her earlier and they were stopping at towns and gas stations on the way here, checking each one. Hasheeba had a feral vampire she was using as a tracker."

Jay frowned. "Huh?"

"Don't worry. Liz will understand. Besides, it's dead now anyway. I killed it."

"Oh."

"And Cassandra's... She's not exactly on our side. But she's not helping Hasheeba any more. Also..." Andreas hesitated and looked down at the weeping wound in his side. "I'm afraid I can't do much more to help you now."

Though he had a bag full of sports drinks under one arm, Jay reached out with his other one for Andreas to lean on. "Well, I'll help you back to the motel then."

Andreas shook his head. "No. I'd just be a liability to you all. Don't worry. Cassandra's getting a car and she's going to get me out of here. I'll be all right. Ask Liz. I've seen worse."

Jay nodded. "Well, I guess... Thanks, Andreas, for—"

"One more thing," Andreas interrupted.

Jay knew by his expression that something was wrong. Well, another thing aside from the myriad of things he was already aware of.

"Matt's dead," Andreas told him. "I'm sorry, Jay."

Portia was in hell. Her mother had been right to ask if she had a fever. She was burning up with one. She rolled one way in the bed, then the other. There was no comfortable position. And fueling her misery was the fact she'd gone off at her mother like that. She wondered if she'd come back if she called her back and apologized. For a moment, she thought it over then decided not to. She felt too embarrassed now and her mom would probably be pretty upset too.

"I should have just let Ivana take me," she muttered to herself. "Saved everyone the trouble of worrying about me."

A voice intruded into her private misery, breaking her out of it. "I'm glad you didn't, Portia."

Portia froze. That wasn't her mother's voice. She turned over and there, sitting over her, was Jay. She smiled at him in surprise.

"Hey," he said. "How are you feeling?"

It was sweet to ask, she knew, although it was a pretty dumb question.

"Like shit, Jay," she told him, deciding to toy with him a little. "I feel like shit."

Jay's lips moved a little as he tried to think of what to say to that. But Portia reached up, with some effort, and put her hand on his—saving him the trouble. "But I'm glad you're here, Jay. Thank you."

Jay tried to smile back but faltered. "Portia, there's something I have to tell you. I just found out Matt's dead."

Tears came again. There'd been too many tears, Portia thought. Maybe that's why she was so dehydrated. For a few moments, she tried to blink them back but decided not to. There was nothing wrong with mourning a friend.

"I'm sorry," she told Jay.

Jay nodded. His eyes were moist as well. "Well, there's nothing we can do about it now. But we can do something about the here and now, starting with getting you well again. Liz—Your mom said you might be happier if I saw you first—"

"Oh, tell her to come in," Portia told him, grabbing his arms. "I want to see her. I want to see all of you."

"Well, Liz and Kyle are outside," Jay said. "But Andreas has—" He gave her a feeble smile then shook his head. "I'll get everyone."

He disappeared and a few moments later, Portia saw them all. Her mom, Jay and Kyle.

"Andreas had to go," Liz told her. "But he's okay. And the rest of us are right here."

Portia nodded and closed her eyes, letting out a breath as she lay back on the bed.

"All right." Liz took over, opening a bag revealing assorted paraphernalia of the medical kind. "Jay, I've asked Kyle already but he can't help here. Do you know your blood type?"

"Sure," Jay said. "I've donated it a couple of times before. I'm O negative, the universal donor."

"Would you be willing to donate it again?"

Having seen enough vampire movies over the years, Jay knew at once where she was going with this. He gave a grave nod. "I'm your man."

Liz smiled. "Well, right now, I need you to be Portia's. Come over here."

Jay did as he was instructed. He knew the drill and sat still while Liz did her work.

When she was finished, Jay felt a little light-headed but he didn't say anything.

Liz put a hand on his shoulder. "I'm sorry, Jay. I feel like I've taken too much. She needed a lot more than I thought."

"It's all right," Jay told her. "I'm good."

Kyle leaned over Portia and frowned. "She's definitely got some of her color back but she still doesn't look well." He turned to Liz. "How in the hell did she lose blood in the first place if Hasheeba can't get in here?"

While Portia's color had come back, Liz's had faded almost in direct proportion. "I don't know. I can't account for it but, clearly, she's not like other vampires." She put her hand under her daughter's head, lifting her. "Okay, now it's time to get her fluids back up. Portia? Sit up, Portia. Wake up."

Portia did so, though her eyes were still closed.

Liz opened a sports drink and put the bottle in her daughter's hands. "Drink this."

Portia sculled the entire thing and dropped the bottle beside the bed. Liz was ready with another one. "And this."

Portia did the same thing again.

Liz then put two ibuprofen capsules in her hand. "Swallow these." Portia did so and Liz passed her another sports drink. "Now drink this."

When Portia was finished, Liz lifted her from the bed. "Good. Now hold on and come with me."

Kyle went round to support her from the other side and they walked together out of the room.

"Let's get her some fresh air," Liz said. "Then I'll give her something for breakfast. Jay, can you get the door?"

Jay nodded, ducking in front. He turned the handle, the door swung open... and everyone stopped.

Standing in the frame, outlined by the dark clouds behind her, was a woman of brilliant beauty and immense terror. Not one among them had laid eyes on her before but they recognized her at once.

She smiled. "There you are."

Liz drew in a deep breath and let it out. "Hasheeba."

Hasheeba gave her an appraising gaze. "Elizabeth Soames. I've been searching for you for a long time. Your reputation has grown considerably over the past three centuries. Yet for all that, it seems you never tried to find me."

Liz wondered how much time it would take to grab her crossbow and come back. With Hasheeba standing here in broad daylight, she wouldn't be fast enough to get anywhere surely.

Kyle, as it turned out, was thinking the same thing. He took a step, reaching out with his free hand to grab the vampire queen—

"Don't bring her in," Liz cried out to his astonishment.

He stopped mid-motion, looking back at her.

"Don't bring her in," Liz repeated, quieter now.

Nodding, Kyle stepped back..

Hasheeba's reaction to this however was almost nonchalant. "Now, now, Kyle," she told him in soothing tones. "That would never do. Aside from bringing me into the one sanctuary left to you, consider what it would look like if anyone saw you—a wanted man—assaulting an innocent woman."

"You're not an innocent woman," Kyle told her through gritted teeth. He frowned in puzzlement at this, staggered by the effort it took to say those simple words.

"And by all rights, you shouldn't be a wanted man," Hasheeba countered, still smiling. "But here we are. Oh—and they're coming, by the way. The police. Or what's left of the Palm Beach precinct anyway. So we don't have much time."

She turned to Jay, looking as though she weren't sure what to make of him, and then to Portia. "Hello, my child."

"I'm not your child," Portia told her through stiff lips. "Or your grandchild either, for that matter."

"But you're Ivana's," Hasheeba told her. "And since she's gone now, you're mine." She turned her gaze back to Liz. "She's dying, Elizabeth. You delayed it a little when you killed Ivana but time is running out for her. Give her to me and I can save her."

Liz set her lips together in grim resolution. "Is that why you came here now? When you're at your weakest?"

"I'm giving you a chance," Hasheeba countered. "I'm giving her a chance." She glanced at Kyle. "And I'm giving him a chance as well. The surviving Palm Beach police who are on their way here are at my command and I can call them off anytime. You can all walk away from here. Alive. Free. I'm making you an offer, Elizabeth." When Liz didn't answer, she spoke again with more force. "Your daughter's dying. Can't you see that? And I'm the only hope she has. Let me take her. Let me do what needs to be done and I can save her."

Then as though she'd stepped out of a deep fog, Liz found it suddenly made sense. Hasheeba was right. Portia was dying. Electrolytes, fresh air and a good breakfast weren't going to do her any good. And stronger measures like medical treatment and even hospital admission wouldn't be enough now. Portia wasn't suffering from a virus. Her malady was of an entirely different kind. And there was only one cure—

She blinked and shook her head, aware Hasheeba was still watching her, smiling. With an effort, Liz resisted her will and reclaimed her thoughts. There was another cure and she knew it well.

She remembered the lonely wet moor. The vicious mob chasing her, their torches glowing bright against the dark sky. What Hasheeba had done to her mother and her father. Her mentor dying in the street. And as the memories flooded over her, she clenched her fists and stared at the vampire queen, thinking how nice it would be to wipe that smile off her face.

"You can't fight me, my child," Hasheeba told her.

Liz shut her eyes and grimaced. "Get out of my goddamn head."

The vampire queen ignored the remark. "A true guardian might stand a chance. But you were never a true guardian, Elizabeth. You may have lived a long life and staked a few of my kind but that's all. Your mentor was twice the guardian you were. His predecessors were the stuff of legend. But the real guardians, I fear, have now all been destroyed. And I should know because I killed them. I found the last of them, if I recall"—her

smile took on a cruel quality that wasn't there before—
"in Seville."

Liz felt her will was almost entirely her own again and
her arms began to move of their own accord. They
moved slowly at first, as though she were tearing
through invisible bonds, but she was no longer
imprisoned by her rival's will.

"You talk too much," she told her. "And you made a
mistake in coming here when it was not your time."

Hasheeba frowned. "I don't think I quite take your
meaning there, Elizabeth."

"Oh, it's perfectly clear," Liz told her. "The sun hasn't
set. It's not even midday. And the hours between sunrise
and sunset don't belong to you."

Hasheeba's lips curled at the edges and her gaze
hardened. "You think so, do you?" Behind her, more
clouds gathered overhead and what light was left in the
day all but disappeared. Gusts of wind whipped up the
sand and the group heard crackling and loud
thunderclaps in the distance. And the sky grew darker
still.

"I don't need to wait for the sunset, Elizabeth,"
Hasheeba told her. "The real guardians knew this. All the
hours of the day are mine."

· · ·

Andreas watched the darkening storm clouds through the window as Cassandra drove.

"It's like one of those tornados you see on TV," he muttered.

"It's Hasheeba," Cassandra replied. "We both know that."

Andreas took a deep breath. Cassandra was right. And yet, knowing that, why were they running?

"We have to go back."

Cassandra took her eyes off the road just long enough to flick an incredulous look his way. "Are you crazy?"

"Liz and the others need our help."

Cassandra nodded. "Right. You are crazy. Look, Andreas. I don't like Hasheeba much and I'm grateful to you for helping me get away from her. Again. Believe me. But that doesn't mean I'm on Liz's side. She hunts our kind, remember?"

"She's always been kind to me," Andreas pointed out.

Cassandra grimaced and shook her head. "No. We're not going back there. If we push it, we can probably get ourselves to the Los Angeles international airport tomorrow night and be back in Europe early next week. Back home. Forget this crass place and that bitch from hell."

"Cassandra," Andreas tried, "helping Liz might be our best—and only—chance of getting rid of that bitch from hell. Look, if Hasheeba leaves the states alive, we'll never be rid of her. She'll find you again and you'll be back at her beck and call."

They drove in silence a little longer.

Cassandra sighed. "Look, Andreas. Let's say you're right. But if we go back, what exactly can we do to help? Any time I go near her, Hasheeba just does something to my head and I can't think straight. And you—you can barely stand. So what's your plan? You're going to bleed all over her?"

"I don't know yet," Andreas conceded, "but —"

A noise that had been faint in the distance but steadily growing louder now drowned out the conversation. And it wasn't the wind.

Looking left, as the cacophony of wailing rose to a crescendo, Andreas saw a train of police vehicles thundering past.

Cassandra slammed on the brakes and, with a screech of rubber on asphalt, dragged the beat-up old car around in a 180 degree swing.

Andreas looked at her in surprise.

"Well," she muttered. "Maybe we can't do much against Hasheeba but maybe we can do something about that."

. . .

Liz, Portia and Kyle gazed at the ancient power before them in horror. Then Jay pushed them back and slammed the door, breaking the spell.

Kyle shook his head. "Wha—?" he managed before he momentarily lost the ability to speak.

"That bitch might be able to manipulate our minds and control the weather," Jay said, "but she can't come in without an invite." He looked at Liz for some backup on this, though he wasn't one hundred percent sure.

"She can't come in," Liz assured him.

A thunderclap so loud it sounded like a bomb going off shook the room.

"But," she added, looking at the ceiling which was still vibrating, "she can still tear this place to pieces or burn it to the ground."

The front door began to creak and bend, pulling at the hinges and threatening to pop them out or snap them. Soon it was an incessant rattling.

"Get back!" Liz shouted. She let go of Portia for a moment and everyone scrambled to the back of the kitchen, crouching for cover behind the counter.

Liz crawled to a cupboard, got out her crossbow and aimed it at the doorway. Then at last, the door flew out over the railing and...

She lowered her weapon. Hasheeba wasn't there.

Frowning, she climbed to her feet and—a moment later—nearly fell off them as another thunderclap rang in her ears and a bright flash filled the open doorway.

There was an explosion. Not a sound like an explosion but an actual explosion. Burning chunks of metal and fumes shot into the air.

"Someone's car just bought it," she said, squinting to see what was happening outside but not daring to go any closer to the doorway.

Jay glanced at the bedroom. "Maybe we try to break through a wall and get into Andreas' room. Or get out through the back of the building."

"Well, we're safer there than we are in here at any rate," Liz said. She nodded to the huddled group. "Go."

They scrambled in, Portia finding new reserves of strength in terror, and Liz went in after them, making sure the coast was clear first.

They heard another noise. Very loud in its own right but muffled by the storm until the source of the noise came closer. But there was no mistaking what it was or what it meant. Sirens.

Kyle looked crestfallen. "At a time like this."

Liz gave him a wry look. "I wouldn't worry about it. We've got bigger problems than them."

Kyle groaned. "But unlike Hasheeba, these guys can come in uninvited."

Liz pursed her lips.

Outside, they heard the screeching of tires on dirt, the slamming of car doors and thumping footsteps on the stairs at the end of the balcony.

Then a voice, distorted by a megaphone but still painfully clear, broke through the din. "Kyle Destri. This is the police! Come out with your hands up!"

The footsteps grew louder. They were almost at the door...

"Stay back!" Liz shouted in her best impression of an American accent, going by the ones she heard most on TV to guide her. "Or I'll kill all the hostages!"

The thudding steps stopped.

Liz glanced at Kyle. "What do you think they'll do now?" she muttered.

"You mean under normal circumstances?" Kyle asked, looking about as despondent as she'd seen him. "Or when they're under the influence of a vampire?"

Liz sighed. "Good point." She ushered the others back and shut the bedroom door. "Okay. Kyle. Help me with this bed."

There were just two beds in the room, the one she'd been using and Portia's. She got on the other side of hers, as it was closest, and—with Kyle—pushed it hard against the door.

"Okay, next one," she told him. "Flip it up and slide it across the top."

There was a commotion on the other side of the door. Whether of their own volition or Hasheeba's, the police were now inside.

Kyle, finding hidden reserves of strength, flipped the bed over himself and shoved it into place. Then, with their barrier up, everyone crouched against the far wall.

"Kyle," Liz murmured. "You don't have a gun with you, do you?"

"It's in my room," he murmured. "But even if I had it here, I couldn't possibly..."

"That's a pity." Liz's expression was grim. "But if there's nothing we can do about it..." She left the rest unsaid.

"Open up!" someone shouted on the other side of the door.

Jay looked around. "We've got to get out of here," he muttered. "Liz, maybe you could shoot a stake at the wall. It might make a hole we can enlarge afterward."

Liz glanced back. "Maybe. But it'd probably make the stake blunt."

"Open up or we'll shoot!"

Kyle gave Liz a worried glance. "I think they mean it."

"I think they do too," Liz said, raising her crossbow toward the door.

"What are you doing?" Kyle hissed.

"These men will kill us," Liz told him. "You know that, don't you?"

"You don't have any hostages..." a voice called back. "Liz."

Liz frowned, pressed her lips together and waited. "All right," she replied, dropping the accent. "But I am armed."

The shooting stopped for a moment and Liz wondered if the police outside were now hesitating about whether or not come in. She gripped the handle of the crossbow harder and...

There was another crack and a hole appeared, just to Portia's right, in the wall behind them.

"Come on," someone urged them.

Without worrying where this newfound aid had come from, the group scurried through at Liz's command and found themselves in Andreas' room.

And Andreas was inside, along with a brunette woman they all recognized.

"Andreas?" Liz asked, stunned and amazed. "How in the world did you —"

"Hasheeba's made it night for all of us," Andreas explained. He nodded to his companion. "Also... Everyone, this is Cassandra." He gave Liz a pointed look. "A friend."

Staring right at her, Liz didn't feel entirely convinced but she lowered her crossbow. "Well, right now an enemy of my enemy is a friend as far as I'm concerned." She turned back to Andreas. "You look like hell, by the way. What's your plan? Because my plan of holding out here's shot to pieces."

As if one of the police officers in the adjacent room had excellent hearing and a particular brand of humor, another shot rang out.

"Literally," Liz added.

Cassandra then took a step back, bracing herself with hunched shoulders. "I'm the plan," she said. She lunged through the hole she and Andreas had made, too fast for the human eye to fully track her. Next, there was a cacophony of shots and screams. Then silence.

Cassandra reappeared, panting and with a bleeding shoulder but otherwise uninjured.

"That'll buy you a little time."

"You didn't kill them, did you?" Kyle asked in alarm.

Cassandra looked at him as though she'd only just seen him. "Lieutenant Destri. Fancy seeing you here. No, I didn't kill them. But I imagine a few of them will have some serious headaches in the morning."

"Hasheeba was controlling them," Kyle reminded her.

"I know. I've been there."

"Where's she now?" Liz asked.

Cassandra shrugged. "God knows."

As if someone upstairs had taken umbrage with her comment, there was a tremendous crack that shook the building to its vibrations and part of the ceiling exploded, showering them with fragments.

Rain poured into the gap and it was now almost too dark to see inside. Whatever lights had been on—which would not have been many since it wasn't even midday yet—were all off now.

For a few moments, the group huddled together further inside Andreas' room.

The wind still shrieked overhead and the rain grew louder but there was no more thunder for the time-being, which might have explained why everyone heard the loud creaks above them...

"She's on the roof," Portia exclaimed, looking up.

"She can't come in," Liz reminded her, although she wondered who she was trying to convince at this point.

Andreas walked to the front door of the motel and opened it without a sound. More light came in—much of it bright blue and red flashes—and though it was nothing close to the brightness of day, it was enough for the others to see by. Yet...

"Andreas," Liz whispered. "What are you doing?"

But he wasn't looking at her, she realized. He was looking at her daughter.

Liz turned to her. "Portia?"

Portia felt a strange sense of calm come over her and when she looked at her mother, she smiled—even as the sounds of Hasheeba's steps grew nearer.

"It's okay, Mom," she murmured. "I know what he's thinking." Without a word, she handed her the book and slid the crossbow out of her hands.

And Liz, despite all her anxieties and fears, all the years she'd dreaded such a moment as this one... let her take it.

Portia looked at Jay. "Thank you, Jay, for everything. You've saved my life twice now."

Whether because he was weakened from the blood transfusion or if it was too painful to say goodbye, Jay just gave her his bravest smile through teary eyes.

"Kyle," Portia said. "Thank you for standing by us. I know you've been through a lot these past few days. It's kind of hard to believe..."

"Thank you," was all Kyle could bring himself to say. He, like Jay, was also moist around the eyes.

Portia then turned back and gripped Liz in a tight embrace. She didn't want to let go and neither did her mother... but *she* was almost at the hole in the roof now. The time had come.

Portia let go and ran to Andreas. The vampire wrapped his arms around her, shot through the door and leapt over the balcony railing.

Below, a dozen or so police officers standing near their patrol cars raised their guns and opened fire. Andreas twisted around, shielding Portia with his body and cushioning her fall.

When they hit the dirt, Portia rolled to her feet and—keeping her head down—sprinted to the nearest patrol car. She opened the door, slid across to the driver's seat and started the ignition...

In the corner of her eye a beautiful but now nightmarish figure, ethereal in the darkness, leapt down from the roof like an agile carnivore on the hunt.

Portia slammed her foot on the accelerator, paying no mind to the dozen shots that hit the back of the car. The dust whirled up as she took off but as it cleared, she glanced at the rearview mirror and screamed. Hasheeba was right behind her...

And she was gaining.

"Did you hear that?" Liz shouted to the others, passing the guardian's book to Kyle and running for the door. "Come on!"

Cassandra jogged beside her while Jay moved much slower, leaning on Kyle for assistance. Unable to wait for them, Liz glanced at Cassandra. "Do you think you can disarm those cops out there without killing them?"

Cassandra hadn't exactly seemed thrilled to be helping her before. And now that Andreas was incapacitated, she seemed even less so. For a moment, Liz was acutely aware that Cassandra's vampire nature could at any moment get the better of her. And that being bossed about by a human might be the perfect thing to trigger it off. And she was also aware that, right then, she was sans crossbow.

Cassandra scowled and Liz braced herself for whatever she'd do next.

"No promises," the vampire muttered. She leapt over the balcony as Andreas had and, keeping low, Liz ran to the stairs at the other end. The sound of deafening gunfire, far louder than the wind and the rain, brought her right back to that hospital tent by the trenches but, thankfully, it was finished by the time she got down.

Soaking wet, obscured by mist and the swirling blue and red lights around them, the cops were standing with their hands up and expressions of bewilderment and disbelief written all over their faces. Cassandra held the only gun now and waved it at them threateningly.

As Liz emerged, one of the cops looked up and shouted. She glanced back to see that Kyle and Jay had emerged.

"Kyle!" the cop yelled, forgetting in the heat of his anger that Cassandra could end his life in a second. "I don't know what the hell you're trying to pull but you're—"

"Shut up," Liz cut him off, "and look around you." She nodded to Cassandra. "You saw how easily my friend here got past you. Well, that's what happened to your colleagues back at Palm Beach. That's what vampires do. And you've just been working for one."

The cop frowned. "Huh?"

"That woman who was here a moment ago," Liz told him. "Now, where did she go?"

Another cop gestured in the direction where Portia and Hasheeba had gone off.

"Thanks." Liz slid into another patrol car just as her daughter did and drove off after them without a word.

Portia hit a road and as gravel and sand gave way to asphalt, there was an instant boost of speed and the car shot away... but not before there was a loud thud on the roof and it buckled above her. Lightning hit a power pole a few hundred yards ahead and it shattered, sending burning fragments everywhere and frying all the others down the road. One fell across her path and she swerved round it, while not letting her foot off the pedal for a second.

But every moment, it was harder and harder.

The darkness, blacker than any night she could think of, compounded her sense of dread and it was impossible to convince herself there were still hours to go before sunset.

The torrential downpour was so heavy now as well, she was for all intents and purposes driving blind. The wipers, swinging back and forth at full speed, couldn't keep up and the windshield was so fogged up anyway that it wouldn't matter if they could.

But worse, she was fading. The new reserves of strength she'd felt after Jay had given her his blood were slipping away. Hasheeba was draining the life from her veins and she wasn't even touching her.

The car rocked to the side and the woman herself slid onto the hood in front of her. With her arms spread wide, she gripped both sides of the vehicle and stared through the glass with a victorious grin—although the enlarged incisors that Portia had imagined were nowhere to be seen.

Still, the sight of this superhuman woman straddling her car and looking right into her eyes was more than enough to stir her imagination. Portia was filled with a primal terror unlike anything she'd ever known. It nauseated and chilled her all at once, clouding her perception of reality itself. And yet, at the same time, she was enamored by Hasheeba's incredible beauty and found herself longing for her to break through the windshield and take her into her arms...

But she couldn't, she knew. Hasheeba could tear the vehicle to pieces but now that Portia had claimed it for herself, she couldn't enter it unless she invited her in. Willingly. Without resisting.

And it seems to me that in her desire to conquer the desires of others, the blood of one who goes willingly to her without resisting would be like poison in her veins.

The words came to her once more and she wondered at them. Did they mean anything? She doubted very much that letting Hasheeba drink from her would poison the vampire. But she had gone willingly to her already, hadn't she? She'd abandoned her mom and the others and drawn her away. And now here they both were, this incredible primeval force and herself, hurtling down a dark and slippery road through a storm that had been whipped up from the depths of hell... and ahead, a slight bend and a wooden picket fence.

Portia slammed the brakes.

The car skidded and swerved and almost flipped over. But a great weight was released and the last thing Portia saw before she lost consciousness was the beautiful demon screaming as she flew through the air.

Liz heard the screech, the shriek of rage and terror and the eerie silence that followed.

The rain still fell but was not as heavy now. And the winds buffeting the car as she drove relented in their attempts to pull the vehicle apart.

But there was no relief for her yet and she felt a knot in her stomach.

She eased off the accelerator and looked as far ahead as she could. Then, coming up to a slight bend in the road, she saw another patrol car crumpled up in a ditch. And beside it, impaled on a wooden fence post, what remained of Hasheeba.

Liz stopped the car and got out.

Hanging limply, with the unbloodied end of the post protruding through her chest, Hasheeba gave Liz a slight smile. But to Liz's surprise, there was nothing malicious in it. There was only a mixture of regret and... pity.

Liz frowned, perplexed by this change in her adversary far more than the manner in which she now found her.

"I didn't want to kill her," Hasheeba murmured, her voice weakening as she spoke. "I wanted to turn her. To make her one of my children." She tilted her head back and shut her eyes. "And now it seems we've both lost."

As she faded and — in the space of a moment — turned to dust and blew away in the wind, Liz knew the world would never see her like again. And knowing full well this was the woman who had taken her parents from her, and who had now most likely taken her precious Portia, she was struck by an acute sense of loss and grief. And she remembered Andreas' words. That Hasheeba would take everything from her if she could and, in return, she'd love her.

The sky was not as dark now and it seemed the blackness, deeper than the far reaches of space, had turned merely to the deepest gray. The rain drizzled now and the wind was a breeze whispering in her ear. None of these things however brought Liz any comfort.

With a heavy heart, she walked to the crashed patrol car and pried the door open. Smoke wafted out of the radiator and the windows were all shattered.

Inside, she found Portia slumped over in the driver's seat. There was a bloody bruise on her forehead as well as several more cuts and scrapes down her arms and, while Liz watched in hope, she drew no breaths.

Being as gentle as she could, she lifted Portia out, slinging her limp arms over her shoulders. Then, with her heart in her mouth, she lowered her onto the ground and felt for a pulse. There was none.

Liz was no stranger to life and death situations. She'd saved soldiers lives in the trenches, and she'd done more nursing since. So she took a breath to calm her nerves and attempted cardio-pulmonary resuscitation for a minute or two but she soon realized the futility of her efforts. Portia remained limp and her skin was cold to the touch.

As the magnitude of her loss began to take hold of her, Liz felt sick. Tears welled in her eyes and she placed a loving hand on her daughter's cheek. Then, as though the gates of heaven had opened, she broke out into loud sobs and clutched her daughter to her chest.

After everything... after all she'd done to protect her...

"Portia," she cried. "Come back. Don't go."

But her daughter, cradled in her arms, gave no answer.

And Liz knew there was nothing anyone else could do for her now. Even if a paramedic were to arrive on the scene, it would still be too late. Her daughter was gone.

Liz closed her eyes tight. There had to be a way.

Then, tentavively, her eyes opened again. There was a way, she knew. One way that just might work. And it was the only thing that was left.

If she wished it.

Liz crouched down, clutching her daughter's hands and put all her thought into the question. The hardest question she'd ever faced. Did she wish it?

For a handful of moments, nothing happened. Then Portia gasped, exhaling a breath and Liz felt something akin to pain. A sense of great loss. And she knew then, in that instant, it had happened. She was mortal again. And in trying to save her daughter's life, she'd inflicted the unthinkable on her. Liz didn't know what to make of it. She now felt the pain of losing her immortality with a greater intensity than she'd thought possible, while at the same time feeling as though a huge weight had been lifted from her. She was wracked with guilt over what she'd done to Portia. And yet...

As Portia opened her eyes and smiled at her, with an understanding gaze and endless love, the other feelings drained away.

It hadn't been what she'd wanted but perhaps, like Hasheeba fulfilling her own prophecy in her attempts to stop it, it was just destined to be. And, as the age old adage went, it seemed to Liz to be the lesser of two evils.

"Mom?" Portia murmured.

More tears came to Liz's eyes, though now they were tears of relief.

She hugged her daughter tight. "I'm here, Portia. I'm here."

Back at the motel, Kyle and Jay ambled over to the assembled police officers, still under Cassandra's steely gaze.

"This is nuts," one of them said, glancing at Cassandra, then Kyle and Jay and then Cassandra once again. "Are we really expected to believe all this stuff about vampires?"

Kyle gave Cassandra a nod. "Try taking her picture and then you tell me." Then, not caring what his former colleagues had to say to that, he crouched by Andreas.

"Hey, Cassandra," he called out. "Let them go. We've got to get Andreas out of here."

The vampire was now very weak. He'd lost consciousness, his breathing was faint and he was riddled with almost as many bullet wounds as he'd taken a century earlier.

Cassandra lowered her gun and came over.

"And one of you men go and check on all the people in the building!" Kyle shouted to any of the officers who were listening. "There's a family in there, not to mention a few more of your colleagues."

The men moved about as though they'd just woken up from a deep sleep and a few of them went up the stairs to check the motel.

The sky was lighter now. It still looked like it was threatening to summon a tornado but it was no longer pitch black.

From the corner of his eye, Kyle noticed one of the officers pull out a camera and take a few snapshots of Cassandra. He smiled as he anticipated the man's expressions of disbelief once he checked the pictures. And he wasn't disappointed.

The smile faded however as he took a better look at Andreas' injuries.

Cassandra crouched beside him.

"Will he make it?" Kyle asked.

"He'll live," Cassandra murmured, though her expression was grim. "But he can't stay here." She hooked an arm under Andreas and lifted him up.

"Here, I'll help you," Kyle said, though he faltered at the wilting look Cassandra gave him.

Then, as though she'd had a small epiphany of sorts, the derisive scowl faded and she gave Kyle a little smile. "Thank you but I think I can manage."

Kyle, with Jay ambling beside him, followed her past the parked patrol cars to an old vehicle of maybe late 1960s vintage, dented all over with visible rust.

Cassandra opened the left rear passenger door and slid Andreas inside. After making him as secure as she could, she shut the door again and turned to Kyle and Jay.

"If the sky's anything to go by, I'd say you don't have to worry about Hasheeba any more."

"I'll believe it when I see it," Kyle replied.

Cassandra shrugged. "Maybe Elizabeth will convince you." She fell quiet for a moment and there was a faraway look in her eyes. "It probably doesn't matter now... But Liz might be interested in this. I knew Hasheeba better than anyone. Better than any other vampire did. And a lot better than any guardian." She gave them both another smile. "It took me a while to figure it out but the truth is Hasheeba was never a vampire. She was a common ancestor."

Kyle frowned. "What's that supposed to mean?"

Cassandra opened the front door and climbed in. "Liz will understand."

As she drove away, Kyle and Jay walked back to the crowd of police officers. The other family that had been inside was now out safe and sound, as were the remaining cops.

Kyle then noticed the smoking wreckage of a car under the balcony.

"Is that yours, Jay?" he asked.

Jay sighed. "Well, that sucks. Still, if that's the worst that happens, I guess that's not too bad."

Kyle pressed his lips together. "I think the jury's still out on the worst thing that's happened today."

He approached his fellow officers, opening his arms in an expansive gesture. "All right, gentlemen. You can take me in now."

The assembled officers exchanged awkward looks and a few of them rubbed the backs of their heads. All in all, they seemed a little sheepish.

"Uh..." one of them tried. "We might need to review some of the facts a little bit before we do anything official. It's been a bit of a strange night.... I mean, day."

"Yeah," another joined in. "And we've still got to look at the station's security footage from the other night."

They shared a few more exchanges among themselves and there were a couple of muted apologies as well. And somewhere in the crowd, Kyle knew, was the man who'd taken several pictures of the beautiful woman who'd disarmed them all at superhuman speed. The assembled officers were all pretty confused right now but that man would be the most confused of the lot.

The sky was beginning to clear by the time Liz got back to the motel. Portia was sitting in the seat beside her, still weary from her ordeal and struggling to keep her eyes open... but she was alive.

Liz saw Kyle and pulled up beside him, winding down the window. "Is everything all right here?"

Kyle nodded and passed her the book she'd given him. He looked exhausted. But then, Liz thought, they all were.

"Jay's just found a spot to lie down out of the way," Kyle told her before hesitating for a moment. "And Cassandra and Andreas are gone. Andreas... He was in a pretty bad shape."

Liz pressed her lips together. It wasn't good news but there wasn't much sense in dwelling on it. "He'll make it," she said. "Although it'll take him a long time to recover. You and I might not see him again in our lifetimes."

Kyle nodded. "I had a feeling that might be the case. But enough about my news. What about Hasheeba?" He looked in the car and saw Portia sleeping beside Liz. "And is Portia okay? What ha—" He trailed off, frowning as something clicked in his mind. "What did you mean by *our* lifetimes?"

Liz turned the engine off. "I have some things to tell you."

She helped Portia over to her own car first and made her comfortable. Sunlight began to pierce through the blanket of clouds, reminding everyone that it was in fact technically daytime. Now, with her daughter sleeping in her car and the thought that they would soon be driving back to Palm Beach, this return to normality in the weather did actually cheer Liz up a bit. However, she was struggling with a sense of unreality.

Was it a dream that she'd passed on her immortality to Portia? And if it was, when was she going to wake up?

Sitting on a wooden fence a little way from the motel, she confided this to Kyle as well as what had happened between Portia and Hasheeba to the best of her knowledge.

"But it was all supposed to happen, wasn't it?" Kyle asked after taking it all in. "You were drawn to Portia.

Someone had meant for her to become a guardian. And she killed Hasheeba, the most powerful—"

Liz sighed. "I know. It's just... That wasn't what I had planned for her. I was trying to protect her from all these things and I failed."

Kyle squeezed her hand. "I don't think you failed, Liz. When the time was right, she knew what to do. You both did. Besides, you can't keep her from the outside world forever."

"I know. But now I'm wondering what happens next. I've changed everything for her. And now I've got to help her find her place in all this."

Kyle waited a moment before replying. "Liz," he said, his voice gentle. "It's time to let her find her own way."

Liz frowned. All this vampire business was completely new to Portia. Until a week ago, she hadn't even believed vampires existed. But, Liz conceded to herself, she had destroyed Hasheeba.

"Perhaps you're right," she replied at last.

They were silent for a little while, watching the clouds clear. There were fire engines in the distance, accompanied by ambulances—no doubt coming to clear up the mess and make sure everyone was okay.

But Liz wasn't planning on waiting for them. Portia was doing all right now and Jay... She looked to her left and saw him sleeping against the fence about a hundred feet away.

She turned back to Kyle. "Is everything all right with you and with your colleagues now?"

He nodded. "Yeah. I think things should be okay there. Although there's a slight downside to all that. Because now the cat's out of the bag. You know, with vampires."

Liz shrugged. "Well, I don't think the cat's gone far. We should be able to keep it contained within the Palm Beach precinct. I'm sure you can convince your colleagues to see the wisdom in doing that."

"Yeah," Kyle agreed. "After everything that's happened this week." He tried to find a lighter subject. "By the way, my colleagues retrieved Portia's guitar from the building. I left it with Jay but it seems to be all right."

"Well, that's something," Liz said, smiling. "She can't spend her life doing nothing but hunting vampires." She then noticed a charred wreck being lifted up by a tow vehicle. "Is that Jay's car?"

"Yeah. It was struck by lightning."

Liz looked at the wreckage a little longer. "Well, I'd better buy him a new one then."

Kyle looked at her in surprise. "That's very generous of you."

"Well, I'd say I owe him," Liz pointed out. "Also, I'm not quite sure how he'd go with an insurance claim."

"Maybe he can talk to the motel owner," Kyle suggested, nodding in the direction of the man in the distance. He was talking to some of the police and, as it turned out, he'd been getting a couple of chores done at home and had missed the whole thing. "He'll have the same problem."

"Well, hopefully your colleagues will help him out," Liz said. Then, since the fire engines and ambulances were closer now, she pushed herself off the fence. "We'd better get going."

Kyle climbed down too. "Yeah. Good idea." He curled his lip as he remembered something. "By the way, Cassandra said something a little odd before she left. Said you might be curious about it."

Liz waited. "Yes?"

"She said Hasheeba wasn't a vampire. In her own words, she was a common ancestor. Does that make any sense to you?"

Liz nodded. Oddly enough, it did. "Interesting."

They walked over to Jay to wake him up.

"By the way," Liz asked, "do you want to get a coffee again sometime?"

Kyle smiled. "Sure."

They made it back to Liz's place by around 8 o'clock in the evening and, since everyone was so tired, it was decided they'd all just sleep there that night. And after showers and a bit of Chinese takeout, they were all passed out from exhaustion.

Elizabeth sat at the table. Her mother and father on the other side laughed at her little jest. With a tender look, her mother passed her some warm bread, while her father went on regaling them both with the excitement of the play he'd seen that day. Tomorrow, he promised, they would all see it together. Content, sitting at the family table with the people she loved, Elizabeth smiled.

Monday

As THEY ATE BREAKFAST AROUND THE TABLE, IT was hard to believe the weekend had been anything more than some fevered dream. They were home again, more or less, and sharing a morning meal like any ordinary family. Or at least without the rushing off to work and college. No one was ready for that yet.

"Where do you suppose Andreas and Cassandra are now?" Jay asked Liz.

Putting down her cup of tea, Liz shrugged. "No idea. Probably on the way home. Wherever home is."

Beside her, there was a distant look in Portia's eyes. "I might see them again though," she murmured.

Liz looked at her, feeling a pang of guilt once more at what had happened. As much as this looked like an ordinary family breakfast, it wasn't. And it wasn't an ordinary Monday morning either. Her daughter was an immortal now as she had been, the youngest in the line of guardians. She'd see Andreas and Cassandra again.

Liz was sure of it. And if Cassandra was right about Hasheeba being a common ancestor, Portia's life was entwined with vampires in more ways than one.

As though sensing her thoughts, Portia reached over and squeezed her hand. "It's all right, Mom. It'll be all right."

Kyle, who had spent the night as well, gave Liz a small smile and got up to wash the dishes. Jay got up to help him, giving Liz and Portia that moment alone.

Liz took a breath and squeezed her daughter's hand back.

After breakfast, while Liz and Kyle were chatting in the kitchen, Portia and Jay sat on the step outside. The street was quiet and dappled sunlight sparkled between the leaves of the trees, making patterns of light and shade on everything in sight.

"How are you feeling today?" Portia asked.

Jay shrugged. "I think I'm all right. I wouldn't want to do that kind of thing every week though." He turned to her, concerned. "But what about you?"

Portia thought about it. "I don't know," she confessed. "Am I a guardian now? Or a guardian-in-training? Have I got some sacred duty to travel the world tracking down vampires? Do I need to start thinking about the practicalities of making fake identities when I hit the age of sixty but still look like I'm thirty?"

She trailed off.

Jay hesitated a little before he replied. "I don't know if my opinion's worth anything here because this is all outside my area of expertise..."

Portia smiled and put her hand on his shoulder. "Hey, it's all pretty new to me too. And don't think your opinion's not worth anything. Go on. Tell me what you're thinking."

This appeared to bolster Jay's spirits a little. "Well," he said, "I think maybe you're overthinking things a little if you're worrying about all that now. I mean, Liz looks great but she doesn't look like a teenager. So I think you've probably got a good ten years or more before you reach the age where you... er... stop ageing. And, if you've got all the time in the world, then I can't see why you'd need to rush into training to be a guardian or traveling the world. Besides, you've had a pretty good start with Hasheeba. Maybe you can have a breather for a few years." He hesitated again, looking a little bashful. "I thought maybe you and I could have a bit of downtime for a while and then, next semester, we could go back and finish our studies." He smiled. "You could make a band maybe. I could teach myself to play drums or something. Possibly bass, if the tunes aren't too hard. We could—"

Portia sighed. "It sounds nice, Jay. It really does. But I don't know if it's a good idea or not. I mean, to get too attached to all of that." Her eyes glazed over a little. "To get too attached to you as well. Or you to me."

Jay frowned. "But we're friends, right? And I thought after everything we've been through, maybe we could... I don't know. Well, you know."

"But it'll end badly," Portia told him, brushing the tears away. "You'll out-age me at some point and eventually, we'll have to go our separate ways. Whether I stay with you to the end or not. I'm even wondering whether I should stay with Mom for too long as well."

"Hey. *Everything* comes to an end eventually. Even for us regular folk who aren't blessed with the gift of immortality. But is that any reason to miss out on all the experiences along the way?"

Portia contemplated this for a little while. "Well," she said, squeezing his hand back. "I guess I could stay here a little while."